"Stop it, Alex," Clarissa said sharply

"Whatever you think, right or wrong, gives you no excuse to behave like this."

His arm went beneath her to cradle her to him as his long, hard body came to rest alongside her, her hurt shoulder imprisoned against his chest. He was kissing her now with the kind of kisses she'd never known existed.

Unable to move in that tight embrace, unable to resist those devastating caresses, she collapsed against him.

What caused him to stop, what caused his head to come up suddenly, she didn't know. But she squeezed her eyes fiercely shut, not wanting him to see the tears she knew were there.

But he said, "Surely not tears, Clarissa."

Mons Daveson remembers sending off her first manuscript after a great deal of work—only to have it rejected. She is now, however, a seasoned author who appreciates the pleasures and frustrations that come with writing. ''There is a certain feeling you get when you start a story,'' she explains, ''a story that has been building, little by little, segment by segment, within the mind, and see the actual words written down.'' It is a feeling of satisfaction once all the sentences and paragraphs finally come together. Mons grew up in the ruggedly beautiful Australian outback, has visited all parts of her country and now lives with her family in Brisbane.

Books by Mons Daveson

Paradise Island
Mons Daveson

Harlequin Books

TORONTO • NEW YORK • LONDON
AMSTERDAM • PARIS • SYDNEY • HAMBURG
STOCKHOLM • ATHENS • TOKYO • MILAN

Original hardcover edition published in 1989
by Mills & Boon Limited

ISBN 0-373-17059-9

Harlequin Romance first edition April 1990

Printed in U.S.A.

CHAPTER ONE

SHE KNEW somewhere within her dreams, or subconsciousness, that there was a noise trying to invade them; then suddenly it was followed by a different sound, the opening of a door.

'Morning tea,' said a uniformed man. 'Townsville coming up in an hour.'

'Oh yes, thank you.' Clarissa took the cup being handed up to her, then turned to glance out of the window at the country sliding swiftly past outside. Yes, the cane-fields were still there, but would be disappearing very soon . . . to begin again after Townsville had come and gone. She drank her tea, then bent over to set her cup on the small shelf.

'I'll get up now, dear, and go to the shower first, if that's all right with you?' came a voice from below.

'That will be fine, Mrs Harrison,' and answering, the girl leaned over to smile good morning at the elderly lady who had been her travelling companion for all the hundreds of miles from faraway Brisbane. She was getting out at Townsville.

But Clarissa wasn't! Lying back, she acknowledged that her thoughts had been right when they had told her that stupidity wasn't the word for what she had done. However, she knew she had had to do it.

Alexis! Her eyes closed, her entire body collapsing at the thought of that name and its owner. Alexis, with the accent on the second syllable, wasn't an Australian name, but the owner of it was as Australian as kangaroo or koala. It had been his grandfather's and father's name too, or so she had been told—from a long-distant past.

She had been only seventeen when she had come up

here to that small sugar town called Ingham which lay on the far side of Townsville. Her mother's friend Ida Smith and her husband owned a cane farm there, and had finally persuaded Mrs Raymond to travel that far north for a holiday.

For Clarissa it had been the start of a wonderful time. Her hostess had told her she could ride the little saddle-horse they kept for the farm; and just having a horse to ride, even if it was only along a river bank and through canefields, was such a wonderful plus for a city girl.

And then . . . oh yes, then . . . she had met Alexis Markham who owned the enormous farm that had to be ridden through to get to the river, and whose far-reaching fields marched away for ever.

Of course young girls got crushes—on seniors at their schools, on film stars, on teachers—but Clarissa, young as she was, knew that what she had felt then was no such thing, even if acknowledging that the image the man presented was what dreams and crushes were made of.

Tall, over six foot, tanned deeply bronze by the far northern sun, with brown hair, bleached fair in places, also by the same sun. With slate-grey eyes, under lids which were often half closed. Oh yes, attractive was his middle name.

Clarissa had never had any crush on film stars or pop singers, but when she had met Alexis . . . It didn't matter at all that he had only been polite when introduced, that her name most likely hadn't even registered. It hadn't registered either the second cataclysmic time.

But before that had happened had come the news. Mrs Smith had gone to answer the phone. She had returned to her interrupted breakfast and gestured with an outflung arm. Looking at her daughter and the two visitors—for it was late and the men were out working the fields—she had said a trifle breathlessly, 'You'll never believe it, Rosie. That was Alexis . . . and he's engaged!'

'Engaged?' Rank disbelief echoed in her daughter's

word. 'He couldn't be! There would have been some sign . . . and,' here she grinned across at the three other women, 'more than a little gossip—as it concerned Alexis.'

'Well, he is. He flew to Sydney and brought his fiancée back with him, to see his home . . . and of course the place where she'll be living. That call just now was an invitation to a dance he's giving to introduce her to the neighbourhood. We're all invited.' Mrs Smith glanced across at Clarissa and her mother.

'Oh, lucky her,' broke in Rosie wistfully, taking no heed of the last sentence, busy with her own reflections. 'She must certainly be a dish of the first water to get Alexis!'

Clarissa only sat silent, but she thought also, Oh yes, lucky you, whoever you are! But not one tinge of jealousy or envy coloured her reflections, because she had never thought of herself in connection with Alexis. He was just someone she had looked at on meeting, and felt a jolting sensation as if every nerve she possessed had been touched with electricity. But she had also accepted that it was something for her alone—and that it would pass.

There was no such sensation where he was concerned. He had turned smilingly away with a compliment that acknowledged her as a charming child.

But he had been so nice, she lay there thinking as the big Sunlander thundered along, her eyes smiling under the closed lids. All the times she had come into contact with him he had been so nice, even if he had treated her as a child. But she had told herself indignantly that she wasn't a child . . . that Alexis was only nine years older. His age she had found out after questions—oh, so casual questions—to her hostess.

And then, on entering the big lounge of Alexis' home, which could almost have been a small ballroom, she had glanced over and seen two dancing forms. That had definitely brought her to herself! It was a scene out of romance—the tall, handsome young man and the beautiful girl revolving slowly to the strains of a band in the far corner.

Because beautiful was the only way to describe Delys. Above average height, like Clarissa was herself, slim but with generous curves in all the right places, unlike Clarissa had herself, she admitted. Gleaming auburn hair clustering about that laughing lovely face, as she looked with enormous brown eyes up at her partner. Clarissa stood quietly at the back of the big room.

But not for long. There were a few youngsters present, and she danced and talked with them in their own corner. Then, at supper, as she was standing at one of the entrance doors gazing out into a scene that these far tropics put on between days of rain, looking at lawns that brilliant moonlight was turning into a sea of silver, at palm fronds, picturesque, beautiful on such a night, sending their romantic image high into the very heavens, Mrs Smith had come to stand beside her.

She said dispassionately, 'It's a sad day that this engagement has come about!'

Clarissa turned, her mouth almost dropped open. 'But, Mrs Smith,' she protested, utterly unable to understand such a remark, 'they look so lovely together—made for each other. Just look at Delys now!' They both turned to look.

And like bees around a honeypot they saw the guest of honour surrounded. Surrounded by men, certainly, but she was acting so nicely, so charmingly, that Clarissa thought that that was a plus; because she had been charming to the women she met as well. Although, now she looked, with her companion's words echoing in her mind, she saw that there were no women at all in that eager group surrounding her.

Then she laughed. 'Really, Mrs Smith,' she answered, 'I'm sure Alexis can more than hold his own against any man vying for her attention!' and her gaze swung to the magnet that was always there for her when Alexis was in her vicinity.

'Oh yes, I quite agree that Alexis can hold his own against anyone. Against men much more attractive than any of those here too.' An arm was outflung to the big room with its laughing, happy crowd.

The dismissing gesture made Clarissa laugh openly, because there were more than a few attractive males scattered about it. But she said, 'Why did you make such a remark about what seems so charming an engagement?'

'Oh, I'm not denying that the girl is beautiful. But beauty is as beauty does, and when two people clash, two people who've both always had their own way, someone is going to have to give in. And that girl over there is going to find out that guileless innocence, spoilt demands, are going to get her nowhere with Alexis. I know him!'

Suddenly a shiver ran up Clarissa's spine at these last emphatic words from such a normally soft woman. Then, young, inexperienced, glancing at the couple across from her who were together again, she said, 'Oh, come on, Mrs Smith—only look!'

Delys was gazing admiringly up at Alexis, the hand on which the big diamond glittered and gleamed placed possessively upon his arm. And Clarissa thought again, with a hurt constricting her chest, that they made a couple that dreams were made of. Impatiently she turned away from the older woman as others came to stand about them.

And then, two days later, on Sunday morning, she was again standing at a doorway, eating, toast and tea in her hands as she gazed outside.

'Well, my lass, are you going windsurfing today?' asked her host, busy with his own breakfast. A big, gruff man, he was kindness personified.

'Oh no, Mr Smith—I wouldn't know how. But that doesn't matter. The rain's stopped, the sun is out to stay, by the look of things, and I love the beach. I'll swim and laze, and thoroughly enjoy myself, thank you.'

The burly man returned to his breakfast and Clarissa went over to the sink to wash her plate and cup, then back to her room. Dressed, she patted in sun-cream and thought as she did so that the long legs issuing from the lemon-yellow shorts were as good as the ones Delys could produce, even if they were a bit skinny now. But that would change. She picked up her shoulder-bag and went outside to join the group already congregated beside the two vehicles—a big Land Rover and a smaller car, both looking the worse for wear.

Speeding through a laneway between endless fields of green and pale jade, Clarissa leaned over and asked the driver, 'Is this your cane, Mr Smith?'

Taking his eyes off the rough track for a brief moment, he spoke over his shoulder. 'It was until a few minutes ago, but from here on, as far as you can see on both sides, it belongs to Alexis. His fields stretch all that way to the main road,' an arm was outflung, 'and on this side they run right down to the river.'

He gave his attention to a particularly rough piece of road for a moment, then said, 'Of course it's enormous acreage, but his family have been here for generations, and they all loved their cane as much as Alexis does. He's probably the most efficient farmer in the district. Oh, look, we cut through this cane-break here, and then out to the main road.'

Clarissa turned her head to look. It was like gazing at a moving sea of green—dull olive at one moment, translucent jade the next, and then, abruptly, a rippling ocean of vivid emerald.

But suddenly, all about them were houses on both sides of the road; low modern brick ones, mixed with the old Colonials raised on their high stilts with the familiar wide verandas all round which had once been needed for coolness. But now, of course, air-conditioning was a way of life.

Passing a spread of large buildings that appeared desolate, deserted, she said to Ned Smith, sitting beside her, 'What are those enormous buildings? I always feel so sad at seeing such places deserted and closed.'

'Oh no, Clarissa!' the voice of the son of the house where she was staying carried shock. 'That's Victoria Mill—the sugar mill. It only works when the crushing starts in June. Then,' he grinned at her, 'it certainly comes alive! A big sugar mill in the crushing season is a wonderful sight. It's a shame you won't be here to see it.'

'Yes, isn't it, but we're leaving in three days, and I'll probably never come back this far north again, or see . . .' Clarissa shook her head, dismissing such unwanted thoughts, and made herself say cheerfully, 'But for this day I'm going to enjoy myself.'

And at the beach as they pulled in under some shade trees she did begin to enjoy it. With golden sand to lie on, a blue shimmering ocean to swim in, and friends to laugh and play ball with, how could she help herself?

It was later, when swimming just beyond other swimmers, that she saw the windsurfer—glorious, a sight to keep and remember, as it skimmed past, its sail of crimson and gold outspread; a tall figure standing upright manipulating it. Then as it passed, it turned and slowed beside her. Clarissa glanced up, meaning to swim back out of its path, when a smiling tanned face gazed down on her and a laughing voice said, 'You're the child from the Smiths', aren't you? Come on up!' And without one thought she raised a hand, which was caught, and found herself swung up. 'Oops—watch out!' Alexis was laughing behind her, as he worked the sail to keep them from overturning.

'Look,' he was telling her. 'You grasp here, and here, and stand there.'

She carefully did as he told her—of course she did. This interlude was something the gods had given her . . . Skimming the sapphire seas, almost flying, she stood with

that tall, assured figure at her back, as the waves parted
for them. 'Look,' the one word came again from above
her head, 'we're a bit far out for you in case we turn over,
so I'll go about. Hold there, and keep still.'

Clarissa held tightly to where he pointed. She kept still;
she felt the warmth of his sun-warmed body cradling her
back as he manipulated the surfer. This I'll always
remember, she thought, as the awareness of him pulsed in
every nerve she possessed, and unconsciously she moved
back a pace. Unexpected movement came as her head
turned involuntarily to look back at him and she found
herself gazing into wide-open startled grey eyes . . . then
they were in the water, the brilliant crimson and gold sail
flat about them.

Clarissa came up as a hand reached out for her. She
said, glancing at the face so close, 'I'm all right.'

But as he returned her look, the man's expression
showed none of the friendliness of before. He cast a brief
glance towards the bobbing heads only yards away, and
said, 'Swim back among those swimmers over there. I'll
get this thing upright.' His face was abruptly turned from
her, his voice now only calmly pleasant. Clearly he
expected her to do what he commanded.

'Yes, OK,' she answered. Then, as he still presented
only a profile to her, she swam away. She didn't see him
watching until she was safe among the swimmers before
he turned to right the big sail and his surfboard.

And he didn't see her, either, cut through them and
walk out of the water. Almost blindly, she moved between
the groups that crowded the beach, and saw thankfully
that Mrs Smith and her mother had disappeared. Picking
up her towel, she turned away from the shade and sat
further down on the hot, scorching sand. She didn't put
her towel down carefully to sit on either: She was
shivering, and she pulled it close about her as if that
gesture gave her protection.

Unaware of the molten rays of a hot tropical sun

playing upon her, she sat wondering what had happened out there. She might be only seventeen, but she had been four years in high school and gone to school dances and outings . . . and had been kissed, even if not expertly. A very much overrated experience, she had told herself wryly, and had decided that work was more important for the present.

Nothing in her life had prepared her for that heart-stopping moment which had occurred out there on the big windsurfer. And . . . another deep shudder rippled through her entire body . . . had Alexis known how she had been feeling? Heavens—he had given a ride to someone he thought was a child staying at a neighbour's farm, a kind gesture to a young visitor—and she had behaved as she had done.

Clarissa's head went down to her bunched-up knees, her fair hair drying quickly in the sunshine cascading all about her. And of course, she realised, there would be only one woman he would be thinking of—his newly engaged fiancée.

As that thought struck at her, Clarissa's head came up, and her glance searched among the crowded beach. Yes, under a very large colourful umbrella, on a very large beach towel, Delys was reclining in the skimpiest of today's fashion bikinis. And she was beautiful! With body oiled and outstretched, she held court, laughing in turn at each of the men grouped about her. Why wasn't she out there on the windsurfer with the most handsome and attractive of any of the masculine figures around? Clarissa suddenly wondered.

To be out there skimming along, feeling like a god—and with Alexis. She cast another glance at the laughing group under the big umbrella. Then her gaze went higher, past the laughing people enjoying the summer day, the swimmers at the edge of the ocean, the windsurfers, searching for a big gold and crimson sail. She saw it, far over and out there on its own. Too far out, she thought. All sorts of things lurked under those innocent-looking waves this far north.

Then she drew her body upright. What business was it of hers? It was Delys who should be watching that flying board. Still, she had had a wonderful holiday; and if she had met a tall, handsome man, didn't every young girl do that at some part of her life? She would put the interlude away to where it belonged, as just a wonderful holiday happening.

So, getting up, she threw her towel over one shoulder and strolled across to where Rosie and Ned were playing beach-ball with the rest of their picnicking crowd.

She played, she ate her lunch sitting cross-legged in her yellow shorts as far away from the Markham party as she could get. She joined in all the games one played at a picnic, and thankfully then settled into her place in the Land Rover for the drive back.

Then, on the day before they were leaving to go home, she saddled the little mare to go for a last ride. Loping through a cane-break with the rustling sugar on both sides, she said softly, 'Goodbye, cane-fields, I probably won't see you again—although I *am* glad I came!' She cantered out as the fields parted, then walked her little horse alongside the river. The sun, low on the edge of the world, sent shafts of horizontal light to stain the water orange and saffron.

Pulling her mount to a stop, she twined the reins to some cane-stalks. Then, walking the few yards to the river edge, she sat down, idly throwing lumps of earth into it while she watched the ripples they created run and speed outwards.

Yes, she decided, she had had a happy holiday, and she *was* glad she had come up here, no matter what! She had not seen Alexis since that lunchtime down at the beach. So she shrugged, telling herself under her breath that she had imagined something which hadn't been there while she was out on that flying board. Oh, well, in less than a week she would be back at school and then on to college, so she would have other things to think about.

Her bent-over figure came more upright as she felt the tremor going through the earth her fingers were playing with. What was it? That rhythmical sound, that deep far-away noise which was filling the air-waves as well as echoing through the earth beneath her? Then she saw the reason for it. From quite a distance away a big black horse was thundering down the river bank. Ridden furiously, it was galloping straight towards her, the pounding hooves sending up the tremor she could feel.

Then the two flying figures, horse and rider, were up to and then past her, and she saw who it was. She saw also, in almost a blur, the reins pulled hard and the horse careering on, unable to stop so abruptly. Then it had turned, and, swinging swiftly from the saddle, Alexis was standing before her.

As it had in the ocean, his hand reached out to her and she was pulled sharply on to her feet. But there was no friendly face smiling at her this time. Clarissa took a step back, actually frightened at this unknown man facing her. His skin seemed to have lost the shining bronzed tan that was so much a part of him. His hair, hatless, fell over his forehead in wild disarray. And his eyes, black and not the usual deep slate-grey, were gazing at her with blazing anger deep inside them. Why . . . why was he looking at her like that, with such furiously blazing anger? She might have strayed on to his land, but everyone used the river. No one owned rivers in Australia . . . so why?

He was speaking to her, the words coming through clenched teeth. 'You little fool! Haven't you more sense than to sit so close to the water's edge, and in such a flat muddy place? All our rivers this far north are crocodile country, and just lately a man was taken only a few hours' run from here.' His hands on her shoulders were shaking her hard, and he said again, 'You little fool!'

Then he was turning her towards her horse. She

went—she had no choice! She had also uttered no words to answer him. What he had said was probably true, but surely a visitor sitting there so foolishly hadn't put him into this towering rage? No, she knew that absolutely! Whatever had caused that had happened before he came across her.

He said, 'Here, I'll give you a hand up,' and bent down to cup his hands for her foot to rest in. His big stallion sidled, causing the reins across his arms to tighten. He was pushed against her, and from bare inches away their gaze met and held. Then suddenly his expression changed. Clarissa couldn't read it, but his cupped hands parted and one went round her back to bring her to him. Then abruptly she wasn't looking into his eyes; her head was being angled back by the free hand upon the nape of her neck, and with his head bent, he was kissing her.

She didn't know how to respond to that bruising, brutal kiss . . . she stayed passive, disbelieving that it was happening. And then, unexpectedly, those scorching lips moving across her own were no longer demandingly hard. They were tender, caressing, as they went back and forth. And clutching with both hands the white silk shirt Alexis was wearing, Clarissa went into the hard, tensile body holding her.

For the space of a heartbeat longer they stood fused together on the river bank, against a sea of green in a darkening evening . . . and then she was being pushed away!

Both hands still clasped on the silk at his chest, she gazed hazily up at him, only dimly hearing him saying, 'I'm sorry . . . I apologise. What else can I say? I only have the excuse that I'm not myself at this moment, so please forgive me. Look!' Again he cupped his hands.

And having no option, automatically Clarissa put her foot into them and was swung up. She went to say, 'It doesn't matter, don't look like that, Alexis,' but he had turned sharply away and she heard the furiously uttered expletive. Then he had swung back, and his face wore a strained smile for her.

He said, 'Off you go home, and please believe I'm sorry I acted as I did.' A hand slapped the flank of her mount and it started trotting at once. It went of its own accord into the cane-break, and Clarissa turned as she entered it. She saw Alexis, mounted now on his horse, both of them motionless as he watched her. She saw them silhouetted against the fast fading light, then the rustling cane hid them from view.

But she heard the flying, thundering hoofbeats, as once more man and beast careered galloping along the soft river's edge. She sat on her own mount, allowing it to have its own way and amble gently along.

Arriving home, sliding carefully from its back, she unsaddled it, rubbed it down, then shut the gate on it. She turned then, leaning back against the old galvanised-iron shed, her legs shaking, still unsteady. She acknowledged that as time went by she might easily have forgotten that blinding look across the windsurfer, but those scorching kisses . . . Oh no!

Only . . . she gave a wry grin . . . those kisses had just started out as kisses to relieve pent-up anger. Deep inside her mind she knew that, and also Alexis had not even called her by her name, not even after . . . when he had been apologising. He probably didn't know it!

But still, a small consoling thought intruded, Alexis Markham wasn't a philanderer. He hadn't the need to be. He was an attractive, a very attractive and very rich cane-farmer. If . . . if there hadn't been that thin tenuous line of chemistry between them which had once surfaced, he wouldn't have behaved as he had . . . wouldn't have kissed a young girl he barely knew.

Giving a deep sigh, Clarissa drew herself upright, then told herself ironically that now she had a special holiday interlude to remember. Except, she also told herself, that this one was too dangerous for her to keep thinking of and she was going to have to wipe it from her mind.

She had found that over the years she had been unable to. That in the five succeeding years of her growing up, going to parties, to the beach, even out on dates, the image of a tall, darkly tanned man coloured all her memories and actions.

So she had decided that if she were to make some sort of life for herself an obsession had to be faced—and destroyed!

At the end of her college training, knowing she was stupid, having told herself so over and over again, she had applied for one of the three schools at Ingham. She had been posted to the one nearest to where the Smiths and Alexis had had their farms.

Her eyes came open, her thoughts disintegrating with the opening of the compartment door and her travelling companion's return. Swinging her legs over the top bunk, she climbed down the little ladder and set about bathing and dressing.

CHAPTER TWO

CASES packed and set down beside her, Clarissa stood in the echoing corridor beside a window, gazing out as the town of Ingham slid past. She remembered it—well, some of it—from her last train journey five years ago, but saw that it had changed and grown. At least on this January day the sky was a welcoming upside-down bowl of translucent blue, when it could have been a pouring overcast arch of grey—for this was the wet season, the season of monsoonal rains. So that at least was a good omen, she decided, pushing from her mind what might not turn out to be a good omen.

At least when applying for the posting she *had* accepted that the man was most probably married by this time; though not to Delys! Mrs Smith had written to her mother about the ending of that engagement, and that Delys had left Ingham the day before Clarissa and her mother had left.

Weeks later, reading that letter, one of the last from Mrs Smith, who had sold out and gone to New Zealand, Clarissa had come to realise that most likely it was the breaking of that affair which had caused Alexis' furious anger.

But even with that on his mind, finding her stupidly sitting on the river bank and realising her danger, he had brought his plunging mount to a stop. And that small diversion had precipitated the event which had changed the whole course of her life. Oh, well . . . now she hoped that actually seeing an older and also probably a family man with children, she would at last be free of the obsession which still made her pulses jump, still caused that tingling, unsettled sensation beneath her diaphragm whenever the memory of him surfaced.

Other passengers were coming to stand beside her now and the train was slowing. Yes, there was the station. She remembered that. And out on the platform, her two large suitcases by her side, she glanced around. It was a busy place with people surging about her, some arriving, others departing, and Clarissa wondered if her headmaster would be meeting her. He had told her that someone would be.

'Miss Raymond!' Clarissa swung round.

A young man was accosting her—well, not a *young* man, but a pleasant one of thirty years or so. She smiled, saying, 'Yes. Are you my boss?'

'No such luck yet, but maybe in a couple of years' time. I'm the deputy head, Peter Graves. George Flower sent me to meet you and take you along to your house.' He was picking up the larger of her cases.

In his car, driving along the wide, beautifully kept streets, Clarissa listened as he explained her work, her billeting, the town and its people. He said, as he pulled to a stop before a low modern house, 'Here's Sarah.'

Clarissa nodded smilingly, saying, 'Hi,' to the girl smiling back at her. Inside, she settled in; she went shopping for groceries with Sarah. On Saturday it rained—no, it poured, a different kind of rain from the sort she had been used to. And on Monday Alice, who owned a car and taught at the High School, dropped Clarissa off to see her headmaster.

After meeting other teachers, being allotted her classes, she stayed back for a minute to gaze around the room she would have for the next couple of years . . . and smiled, a small tingle of excitement going through her. It would be great to start work, to begin earning money. And now, being actually here, she realised how silly had been the reason for her coming. When she met Alexis—if she did meet him—she decided he could well be someone she would not even recognise! A vastly different man from the one lodged in her memory.

She gave a last glance over her shoulder, then walked through the door. Not looking, she almost bumped into her boss, and as she gazed up at him with a smiling apology, the smile went glazed, her body rigid. It simply couldn't be!

'Oh, Clarissa,' her headmaster was saying, 'this is Mr Markham of the P and C committee. He may not have any children here, but he does live in the locality, and we find him very useful when we want donations, don't we, Alexis? Our new teacher, Miss Raymond.'

The man was looking at her. He smiled . . . and every bone in her body melted. He said, and the word slurred, 'Clarissa . . . yes!' And turning from her, he told his companion, 'I think I've met Miss Raymond before, a long time ago.' He turned back to her and an eyebrow rose. And deeply back in those slate-grey eyes a spark glowed . . . a diamond pinpoint of light.

If he thinks he's going to have fun with me, he has another think coming! Clarissa reflected wrathfully. I'm not a schoolgirl any longer. She told him politely, 'Yes, I think that may be so, Mr Markham. You had a farm next to friends of my mother, if I remember rightly.'

The diamond pinpoints grew brighter, but the smile he was returning was also only polite and casual.

Clarissa turned, using the same politeness as she said, 'I'll be off, then, Mr Flower. Thank you for all your advice. Mr Markham!' She nodded a careful smile at both men and walked away.

But Alexis had raised a hand to her boss in a departing gesture, and turned to accompany her. Taking no notice, Clarissa hurried on. 'Here, be careful,' a voice said, a soft voice that she remembered, and a hand came out to clasp about her arm. 'You're not a child now, you know, running about in sneakers,' the amused voice from above her was continuing. 'You'll go tumbling down those steps if you race down them in those shoes.'

Unable to free herself from the grip of those strong fingers, Clarissa had perforce to slow down. She *was* wearing very high-heeled shoes, because she had dressed to meet a new headmaster, thinking that the brown linen skirt with a thin lemon blouse was just the kind of outfit this occasion warranted.

Again she tried to free her arm before saying, 'As you said, Mr Markham, I'm not a child now, and I really can navigate steps, high-heeled shoes or not. But thank you for helping me, and goodbye for now.'

'I'm going your way, I'll give you a lift,' was the only reply she received.

'No, thank you just the same. I have someone meeting me.'

'Have you indeed?' Suddenly that soft voice from beside her wasn't carrying amusement any more. It had gone crisp and curt. 'In so few days?' it was saying. 'You certainly have grown up!'

'Oh, there they are.' Thankfully Clarissa saw that Alice's car had just pulled into the kerb. She turned, and actually facing her companion for the first time she found, gazing at that tanned handsome countenance, looking into those deep grey eyes, that the dismissing words she had been about to utter had disappeared.

They stood, immobile, gazing directly at one another, and as it had done once before across a flying windsurfer, a line of tension stretched between them, unseen, but as palpable as a line of stretched electricity.

Turning abruptly away, Alexis moved along to the gate, holding it open for her. He also reached out to open the back door of the car waiting there, leaning down to smile at the front seat passenger who was so frankly laughing up at him.

'Hello, there.' He was answering her greeting, and in the back seat Clarissa thought astringently that he didn't remember Sarah's name either.

But he was being told. 'I'm Sarah, Mr Markham. We met last year!'

'Oh?' An eyebrow went up, and that soft, amused voice wasn't only amused this time, it was laughing. He said, 'A very famous name these days . . . congratulations!'

'Yes, isn't it just!' Sarah was laughing up at him as she answered. 'And like Sarah Ferguson, maybe . . . just maybe one can use her as an example. She snaffled the most handsome and eligible male around. I might be able to make it my moment too, as there are other handsome and eligible males around to be snaffled, so . . .'

There was no mistaking her meaning, and Alexis smiled down at her. 'You could be right,' he said. 'But as I'm only a poor cane farmer, I'm afraid I'll have to pass.' His teeth flashed white in a bronzed face as he raised a hand, smiling impartially at all three of them before adding, 'But that doesn't mean that maybe, just maybe, we couldn't all meet again.' He swung round, and suddenly he wasn't there any longer.

'You're just too much, Sarah,' said Alice quietly. 'To act like that! What in the name of goodness must he think of us?'

'He would think, as every other attractive man would think, that I was making a pass at him . . . which I was. Too bad that he let me know—in the most polite way, of course—that he wasn't interested.'

'I should think he wouldn't be! Young school teachers aren't in his league. However,' Alice paused as she negotiated the turn into their own street, 'I know someone who thinks she is, or hopes she might be.'

'Goody. Tell us!' Sarah swung round animatedly.

'As you know, Eddie works for the hospital, and Mr Markham is on the hospital board as well as on your P and C committee. At the end of last year he gave a dinner party at a big restaurant in town for some of the hospital staff. I went—and so did Dr Lesley Armitage.'

Clarissa withdrew her attention from the scene outside, sending a quick glance at the two girls in front. The one driving was adding, 'Eddie did say, however, that Mr Markham has a fabulous room at the front of his home to entertain in—almost a ballroom, and . . .'

Clarissa interrupted, asking carelessly, 'You talk about the man's parties and about him making passes, but he's on a school committee. Isn't he married? Doesn't he have children?'

'Oh, no!' the reply came quickly from both girls. Then from Alice, 'His property begins on this side of the town, and being public-spirited, and very wealthy, he's co-opted on to every committee that can grab him.'

'But what about this Lesley Armitage? This doctor . . . Alice?' Sarah was only interested in the man, not in his community help.

'That . . . well yes, I expect you could say that if anyone could be said to be in his league, it's our newest hospital doctor—from a socially prominent Townsville family, beautiful, clever and, if I'm any judge, knowing exactly what she wants.'

'Oh.' Clarissa retreated into silence. Because she wasn't going to say that she had previously known Alexis and had also been to a party at this house they had been talking about. That information would bring all sorts of questions down upon her head. And Alice had not mentioned anything about a broken engagement . . . or Delys.

Slipping from the car as it came to a halt in the garage, she stood gazing over the pleasant, modern house, not looking at it with proprietorial pride as she had done on the outgoing journey, happy to be billeted there. Now . . . now, she realised, it hadn't helped her to come up here—in fact, the reverse.

She had come all these hundreds of miles to obliterate a man's shadow which had overcast any and every attempt to make a life among her peers. She had thought she would see him . . . oh, yes. In a small town like Ingham, of course she would. But across a street, or even one day to actually meet and say hello . . . and that then she would be able to smile, and laughingly acknowledge that she had made a dream of only a memory! It had not happened like that. She *had* met him—on her third day here!

But, following the others up the steps, she knew it wasn't the ghostly memory of Alexis that mattered now. It was the real live man! And a man, too, who had looked at her with only laughter in his eyes. Who no doubt now thought of her as just a young schoolteacher instead of a visiting youngster—with probably only a blurred outline remembered of that love-scene on a darkening riverbank.

Life went on its journey, as it has a habit of doing. Clarissa found her way around work and lessons. She took her one week in three of cooking meals and doing the shopping. Alice drove them to school of a morning, for which Clarissa thankfully paid petrol money.

She walked home if it was fine, and caught the school bus when it rained. She received her first fortnight's cheque, and thought she was a millionairess.

Then one Wednesday, after she had been at Ingham for almost a month, their headmaster walked into the staff-room during one lunchtime. 'Alexis Markham is giving a barbecue on Saturday evening and we're all invited. Give me your names so I can let him have them by Friday.'

'Don't be funny, boss. Just count noses! I can't imagine anyone not going. It will be the best turn-out we'll ever be invited to—if I know Alexis, and I do . . . well, a little bit.'

Jerry grinned round at all the faces. He was a native of this place, and back from college, had only been teaching for two years.

Glancing around in her turn, Clarissa thought he would probably be right, and wondered what she herself should do, knowing, of course, that without a valid excuse it would be wondered about if she stayed away.

CHAPTER THREE

AND OF COURSE she was going. So now Clarissa gave a last contented glance into the mirror. Yes, she was satisfied. She might not be outstandingly beautiful, like Delys, or like this doctor Alice had mentioned. But yes . . . her honey-blonde hair, just shampooed and blow-dried, hung about her face and neck, the fringe cut straight across her forehead.

Her eyes, only an ordinary blue, not the shade of cornflower or sapphire one sometimes saw, showed tonight almost lovely with the eyeliner and eye-shadow she had used with a generous hand. She smiled back at her reflection, because her other good point besides her hair was her teeth which could have been used for a TV toothpaste commercial.

She swung round to leave, and felt the stiff cotton of her dress curl about her bare legs, then glanced up as a tap came on her half-open door. Sarah walked in, saying,

'Have you got a nail-file, Clarissa? I've snagged one of mine and I don't want to break it.' Then she looked more closely at Clarissa.

'Wow!' she exclaimed. 'You look as if you'd just stepped from a fashion magazine, and . . .' her tone changed, echoed tartly, 'don't start telling me again that you were poor and got all your clothes at sales-time! I've never seen one outfit of yours which didn't look as if it hadn't come from some exclusive boutique—and that one . . . Good heavens!'

'Yes, it is nice, isn't it?' answered Clarissa smugly, pirouetting. But the dress she was wearing didn't fit such an insipid description as 'nice'. Cut from golden yellow cotton, it had a zig-zag stripe of pale jade beginning from the low scooped neckline down to the tight waist, then continuing on down the swinging skirt to the hemline. It was a creation!

'But,' she was continuing, 'I did speak truly when I told you my mother worked in the dress section of the largest department store in Brisbane, and that she used to watch when the sales began. I *was* one of the poorest girls at school, but I expect the way I dressed—even my school uniforms —made me one of the best-dressed girls there. My mother has a very good dress sense, you know. This one *is* nice, isn't it?'

'It's fabulous! Looks like a model creation, and yet it's so suitable for a large barbecue. And your hair, of course, looks as it always does, perfect . . .'

Clarissa interrupted. 'You say that, Sarah, I know. But it's only a long pageboy bob, and I've always worn it like this because it's so easy to handle. I've never had a style-cut in my life—we simply couldn't afford one. Just a hairdresser to cut the ends and my fringe when it grew too long. We really didn't have any money for frills. Now you . . .'

In her turn, Clarissa looked Sarah over, at that hair, coloured to resemble another Sarah's, and which was certainly style-cut. 'Now you,' she repeated, 'I expect have had that lovely hair style-cut since you grew up.'

'Oh, even before that,' replied the irrepressible girl facing her. 'Just after I started high school, I expect. Around twelve or thirteen. And also I had all my frocks bought for me—and not at sales-time either! But I never look like you do, Clarissa . . . as if you'd just stepped out of a famous boutique and out of an even more famous beauty salon.'

'Oh, come on, Sarah, don't be silly!' Embarrassment echoed in Clarissa's reply. 'I probably spend a little more time co-ordinating my clothes—because I've had to. But I'm afraid that beside your outgoing personality, I'm cast in the shadows.'

It was Sarah's turn to smile a little smugly now. She was wearing white, low-cut and strapless. Thinly trimmed with navy, it also looked what it was—an original, and, suspected Clarissa, bought just for tonight's event. Its perfect white simplicity was the very thing to set off the elaborate chestnut-red curls clustering about her face and the red-lipsticked mouth from which smugness had departed, allowing a confident expectation to take its place.

Picking up her small evening purse, Clarissa walked over to switch out the light, and they found Alice waiting for them at the front door. 'Oh, here you are,' she greeted them. 'I was just going to call you. Eddie has arrived. Shall we go?'

And in the car, after introductions to the other young man there, Clarissa thankfully let Sarah begin working on her first conquest of the evening, and settled back on the other side of Stan. All *she* felt, now that the time had really come, was a sick feeling of apprehension.

She knew she shouldn't feel it. She knew she would probably only receive a smiling greeting from the host of tonight's affair. Of course she would get that! Alexis would be nothing if not a polite host. But . . .

She absently answered a question, then their vehicle had turned off the main road and on to a short gravelled driveway. A young man was directing cars into a parking lot. He came across to them saying, 'Hi there. I'm Jim Henson, car-park attendant for tonight. OK, just over there.'

Eddie pulled in to where he was directed, and getting out of the car, they followed a group just ahead. Alexis was waiting to greet his guests. He looked their party over and said, 'How lucky I am to see my barbecue graced by three such lovely young ladies!' He nodded casually to the two men, smiled charmingly at Alice, and looked the other two girls up and down.

He laughed at the open invitation he was receiving from Sarah, then turning to Clarissa, he said very softly, 'You've certainly grown up! Our little community welcomes you back!' And before other comments could be made, before he could see the warm colour abruptly staining her cheeks, he was shepherding them across to where the headmaster and other members of the school staff were standing, drinks in hand.

Once again they were looked over, but so differently this time. George Flower said, 'Look at this other addition to my staff which I've been given, my dear,' and went on to introduce Clarissa to his wife.

Clarissa liked her, finding her comfortable to be with and willing to be friendly. This turned out to be the same with Eileen, the deputy's wife, too. She turned when a well-remembered voice said, 'I hope that what I've brought meets with your approval. However,' Alexis' laughing words continued, 'you can always dispose of them and re-order. The bar's over there!'

Glasses were handed round—beer for the men, a glass of wine for Alice, and what looked like fruit punch for Sarah and Clarissa. In the jumble of conversation and laughter passing through the whole garden and barbecue area, other softly spoken words passed unnoticed. 'But you're not *that* grown-up!' as she was handed her fruit punch.

'Isn't it just Alexis' luck to have been allowed such a glorious night for his party?' someone was saying. 'No rain, and a clear sparkling star-studded sky.'

Glancing up into a velvet canopy pierced with glittering diamond pinpoints, Clarissa didn't take in the rest of the talk and laughter. She was remembering another scene at this very house, one taking place in the ballroom inside; remembering another night which had not been dark with brilliant stars, but shimmering with bright moonlight which etched the shadows of feathery palm-fronds across a sea of silver lawns.

She shivered as someone touched her arm and spoke, bringing her thoughts sharply back to the present. Making herself join in with all the appearance of thoroughly enjoying herself, she watched under downcast lashes the tall figure of Alexis moving among his guests.

He wasn't at the cooking area, where a busy cook was

preparing steaks which were already wafting their tantalising aroma across the air-waves. He was pouring a drink, smiling down at a woman as she held out her glass.

Clarissa sighed, thinking she had decided that being dressed as she was made her for once someone who might catch eyes or make heads turn. But as a swinging coloured light caught Alexis in its glow for a brief moment, she thought wryly that it was *his* image that dreams were made of.

Looking at him—tall, completely assured, clad in grey trousers and a silk shirt of the same colour which had to be handmade, with teeth gleaming white against tanned skin as he smiled, she wished suddenly that it was her that he was smiling at so charmingly.

Then, even across the rising noise of a party getting into full swing, she heard his voice that spoke so softly for such a big man, and again a shiver passed through her, as she remembered an occasion when it had not been soft, but fiercely angry . . . remembered a face not laughing as it was now, but violently angry as it leant over her. Remembered scorching kisses . . . Her hand jerked as someone bumped into her, and she held her drink tighter.

Alice leaned over and whispered, 'Here's the beautiful doctor!'

Clarissa's glance, moving swiftly to the entrance of this area, saw four people arriving—and also saw that tall figure moving past her own group to go forward to meet them. The other three members of the new arrivals didn't register. She only saw a small woman, petite and looking quite lovely—but not nearly so beautiful as Delys had been, then, with a wry grin surfacing, Clarissa acknowledged that very few women would be as beautiful as Delys had been.

But this one was lovely in an altogether different way. She looked a poem in white. Though where Sarah's hemline stopped only inches below her knees, the newcomer's skirt, longer than the present fashion, was a swirling flare with a large stylised black rose blazingly sprawled eye-catchingly across it.

Her hair, as black as that rose, was worn smoothly in a shining cap, with just two smooth wings lying against her cheeks. As she stood, one hand lying possessively on Alexis's arm while she was being greeted, her head came just to his shoulder.

Moving in a group, they were coming in this direction, stopping to chat occasionally on their way. Clarissa moved back a little as they halted before their small crowd. There were introductions from a charming host; there were casual hellos and nods. And Clarissa stood, smiling a little, as she eyed the glance passing between the two attractive women in their beautiful white dresses.

Sarah would be furious, and she guessed that this Dr Lesley—somebody would be too. Cool politeness was the only gesture they were exchanging. Both spoiled, Clarissa surmised, both used to getting their own way . . .

Then something, some different air-wave, brought her attention completely from them, causing her to look up. She felt a jolt go through her.

She found herself gazing at a man who was looking directly at her. The tiny smile his lips held, the knowing look, told her he was aware of the thoughts coursing through her mind about the two women standing between them, and that he echoed her reflections.

But she straightened up as she smiled only politely while nodding at this man Alexis was introducing as Fred something or other, and to whom the irrepressible Jerry was saying, 'Hi there, Federico!'

He was dangerous, this man, someone to keep away from, went her thoughts. And yes, he *was* a Federico, although he looked more Greek than Italian or Spanish. And . . . this jolt tonight brought recollection of another such jolting shock she had received when gazing suddenly at a different man—on a windsurfer. That one, however, in no way resembled tonight's occasion.

From Alexis, kindness had always been the predominant

attitude—except for that one event! But with this man, this big dark man with skin that showed a different shade from the bronzed brownness of the man standing beside him, with an expression in his tawny eyes which would not have shamed a lion stalking his prey—oh no!

Clarissa glanced quickly away, and in doing so met another look—from a face that had been in her memory bank for years. But it hadn't carried this sort of expression. Alexis' face now could have been carved from stone, the eyelids half shut, indented lines about a mouth which was normally a smiling one. Startled, her glance took in that ruthless face—because that was all she could call it—and a shiver went through her entire body.

Then they had all moved away, and Alexis called over a shoulder, 'Jim!'

Young Jim Henson moved across to him and listened to a murmur of words for a few minutes. Then back with them, casually waiting for a few seconds, he spoke softly in Jerry's ear.

That young man then collected his own partner, Sarah and Stan, and two other girls from the group, and gesturing Clarissa before them, was saying, 'Alexis said to go down to the other end where the tiles are smooth for dancing, unlike these cobbles. Come along!'

'Wouldn't it just?' murmured Sarah bitterly. 'And I went all the way to Townsville for this frock!'

'Oh, come on, Sarah,' Clarissa said a little impatiently. 'What does it matter? You both look fabulous, so why worry? And I expect you'll get more than your share of masculine attention in it tonight.'

She followed her companion's glance then and saw the host of all this speaking, not to the attractive Lesley, but to a group of senior men only a few steps away from themselves.

But then his form was obscured as Jim joined their small group with both a couple of extra men and the sound of dance music. In the flurry of laughter at finding partners, Clarissa suddenly found hard fingers on her arm and herself being whisked behind a clump of thick-foliaged oleander trees.

She knew whose fingers they were—of course she did. But her hand went up to disengage them. It was a wasted effort. She said, 'What are you doing, Alexis? Let go of my arm!'

'When I've told you why we're here! And that is to keep away from the vicinity of Fred Martinez. He's not the sort of man for you to become involved with!'

'Are you mad? I've only just met the man! I've only said two words to him!'

'I realise that! But sometimes words aren't necessary. Looks and atmosphere convey a whole lot more.'

Clarissa nearly said, you should know. But with a quick glance at the face, ruthlessness showing on its every plane and angle in the shifting, swinging light, she didn't. She said instead,

'I think you must have been drinking your own party mixture, and it's gone to your head!'

A low laugh, cold, arctic, interrupted what she had been about to add, and Alexis told her, 'Oh no, my dear Clarissa. When you get to know me better you'll learn that drinking is not one of my vices. It's not one of Fred's either. But he has others. So . . . understand this, because I mean it! You keep right away from him and refuse any and every invitation he extends.'

'Oh, really, Alexis!' Clarissa's voice didn't hold icy chilliness, but it did hold astringent amusement. 'Why should he send me invitations? As I said, just two words are all we spoke together. And . . .' again trying to shrug off those hard fingers and finding herself unable to, she added tartly, 'And after all, I met him here at your home. Why is he here if he's so unacceptable?'

'I didn't say he's unacceptable. I've known him for always, and he's a good mate . . . on a fishing trip, a jaunt to Brisbane to attend sugar conventions, but I didn't invite him here tonight, and usually he wouldn't have come, even if I did. This sort of affair isn't his scene; he normally spends his free social time in Townsville . . .'

It was Clarissa interrupting this time. She said disdainfully, angry at this scene, 'Well, what he does, and what you're saying, is of no interest to me. Let go of my arm and I'll return to the people you do think are my own sort!'

'You little fool!' A nostalgic sweet memory of an interlude on a river bank swamped both her and this angry scene for a brief moment. Those same words she had heard before; and now, as on that time too, he was shaking her, as he repeated, 'You little fool! I saw the way he was looking at you, and with Fred that means only one thing. Oh, you might not be interested, but he certainly is. So I'm warning you, Clarissa . . .'

Answering that arctic voice which carried so much more chill for being kept low, she said, 'Why not give the same advice to Lesley Armitage? After all, he came with her.'

'I don't need to tell Lesley Armitage anything. I should imagine she'd know how to handle him—whatever his intentions are there. She's a doctor and has probably met all sorts of people, in all sorts of places. I haven't got to worry about her. But you . . . In the normal course of events most likely you would never meet him. As I said, he doesn't spend much of his leisure time here. But as you *have* met him, and here at my home, I'm telling you, and I mean it, refuse any invitations you receive from him. Understand me, Clarissa!'

She found she was released, and that an inimical presence had departed around the opposite side of the oleander clump. Falling back a step, her shaking fingers now clasped tightly over the area other fingers had just left, she felt her face touched by soft velvet. She knew what it was. Its sweet, pungent fragrance had been all about them as she and Alexis had stood, so close together, but in so angry an atmosphere.

She knew now, inhaling the perfume of the spray of flowers touching her cheek, that she would always associate the vividly sweet smell of oleanders with Alexis in a cold rage. She knew he had been right! That man Fred, or as Jerry called him, Federico, *had* looked at her differently.

However . . . inhaling deeply of the warm scented air about her, Clarissa knew that there had been no need for Alexis' warning. She would no more go out with Fred, with someone she had thought dangerous after one swift glance, than she would ever again sit on the edge of a muddy river bank.

She heard Sarah's voice calling, so with one set of fingers still clamped around her other upper arm, she broke off a spray of flowers, then strolled out in the opposite direction to the one Alexis had taken. 'I couldn't resist them!' she exclaimed, showing her booty. 'Aren't they lovely?' They were as good an excuse as any other for being missing for a minute or so.

Jim, standing beside Sarah and Stan, laughed. 'Yes, I expect they are, and they certainly are a sight around this area when they're all in bloom, but they're so common we hardly notice them. Come and dance, Clarissa.'

So she went and danced, and not only with her own small group. Her boss came along and happily she danced with him, and remained away thankfully from the vicinity of Alexis and Lesley and Fred.

The time for eating what the delicious aromas were wafting all about them came along, and again it was Jim helping her to collect steak and salads, but she waved away other meats from the cook, who was his father. They went, accompanied by the rest of the younger crowd, back to the small dance floor with the wide, curved cement wall enclosing it.

CHAPTER FOUR

'HERE, let me,' said Jerry, who, with hands placed under the arms of his partner, had swung her up, and now jumped Clarissa too on to the wide surrounding wall. They all ate and told stories and set about thoroughly enjoying themselves.

And a little sadly Clarissa thought once again how lucky she had been to land here in this town—to a good teaching job, a good boss, nice girls to live with—and all of it was dust and ashes, because . . . Her eyes lifted to see the reason for that fact. The host of all this, glass in hand, was wandering among his guests, replenishing their drinks, having a few words, a laugh, before wandering off to another group.

Jerry had disappeared for a few minutes and then he was back with a wide grin. 'Knowing my way around here,' he told them, 'I've snaffled us some baklava before it all goes. There are tons of Australian desserts, but I like this Greek stuff. If you don't want yours, Clarissa, I'll eat it.'

'Oh no, you won't! I'm going to Greece one day, and there's no time like the present to get accustomed to things I might meet up with there.'

Clarissa ate the delectable concoction slowly, sipping at the glass of wine Jerry had procured for her, as she sat, silent among the chatting people.

Then, as Jerry was minus his partner for a minute, she turned, asking him as he was sitting on her other side, 'Who's that man with Lesley Armitage?'

Fork poised, Jerry took a moment to glance around. He laughed, saying, 'Keep your interest far away from him, Clarissa. He's not for young girls like you! That's Fred Martinez, or actually, Federico Martinez. He owns a large cane farm on the other side of town from here, but he doesn't mix in with the social life in Ingham very much. He mostly spends his free time in Townsville—his extra-curricular time, I mean.

'He does go on fishing trips, shooting expeditions and so on with his friends here, Alexis and my older brother among them, but . . .' Jerry broke off and began to eat.

'I can't understand you, Jerry. Anyone would think . . .'

'Look, Clarissa,' the interruption came curtly, 'Fred's a good bloke, but like Alexis, he's had too much money all his life. However, he's put his to far different uses. Just don't get interested in him, that's all. His mother is a Greek and a lovely lady, but Federico . . .'

'Greek? I would have thought Martinez was Spanish.'

'It is. His father was Spanish. Right, love?' The last two words were directed to Jerry's returning partner, and other matters of conversation were dismissed.

They carried their empty dishes to the bench beside the barbecue fire, then sauntered back over close-cut lawns that sprang velvety and smooth under their footsteps, with tree branches high above, whispering in a warm breeze that had just sprung up.

Back at their little dance floor, Clarissa stood with Sarah, idly watching a couple trying out steps in its centre, when abruptly, among a group of older men discussing cane, one of them stumbled. As he flung out an arm quickly for balance, his glass of red wine splashed widely, right across the skirt of Clarissa's dress, soaking it.

Aghast, she stared down, shock at its ruin making her unable to speak for a moment. Then she said without being aware she was saying it, 'Oh, my lovely dress!'

Then glancing at the man returning her look, seeing on his face the same degree of mortification which her own must be showing, she forced herself to speak. 'It doesn't matter. It was an accident.'

Then all was movement about her. The unknown man was saying apologetically, 'Look, my dear, I'm sorry. I'm so

sorry . . .' when a curt crisp voice intervened. It was asking,
'What in the . . .?'

Clarissa found herself glancing up into bleak, dark grey
eyes, and said again, her own voice going curt too, as she
took in the girl standing by Alexis' side, whose careless smile
said all she was thinking, 'I've said it doesn't matter, and it
doesn't. Forget it!' Then turning to Sarah, she added,
'Could you find Alice or Eddie for me, please?'

But a curt dismissing gesture had halted Sarah as she
began to move, while Lesley was saying with amusement,
'Good heavens, she looks far worse than some of the accident
cases we get in to patch up on a Saturday night!'

The voice which answered her held no amusement at all,
and even in her distress Clarissa thought suddenly that she
wouldn't like that voice speaking to her in such a tone.

'Let's hope then,' it was saying, 'that you can attend to
them just as easily as I can attend to this.'

Alexis told the man who had bent down to pick up his
fallen glass, emptied of its last red drop, and who was still
trying to apologise, 'Forget it, mate. What's a little accident
between friends? Keep your worried frown for something
that needs to be worried about.' A smile passed between
them.

'Stay with Clarissa, Sarah,' said Alexis then. 'I'll be back
in a minute.' He was moving away with a peremptory hand
on his partner's elbow that guided her swiftly to a small
group further down the garden.

He was back in that bare minute he had mentioned.
'Jim,' he said, 'get the youngsters dancing, and then see
about refilling drinks. Your mother is kindly taking over
while I'm gone. I'll only be ten minutes. Come along,
Clarissa.'

'There's no need for you to leave,' Clarissa protested. 'I
know I have to—my skirt is dripping wet. But Eddie will
drive me.'

Those deep grey eyes were still showing almost black as
they returned her look, and the sculptured lips thinned. A

different face gazed back at her. He said again only, 'Come along.'

Her arm was taken as it had been once before tonight, and just as tightly. She went along.

The Jaguar was sitting waiting before the big, wide front steps; the passenger door was opened while the owner of the vehicle waited politely, silently, beside it.

Clarissa gazed down at her wet, deeply stained skirt, then, shaking her head dismissively, gathered it about her and stepped inside.

'I'm sorry about this, Clarissa,' Alexis said as he sent the car down his right of way on to the main road. 'Such a stupid accident, and your lovely frock ruined. I expect your night is as well, and you seemed to be enjoying yourself.'

'Yes, I was enjoying myself, thank you. It was a great party. But as you say, accidents can always happen.'

'Maybe they can, but I would prefer them not to happen at *my* parties, or at *my* home.'

A shiver passed through Clarissa as she sat squeezed up in her corner, endeavouring to keep her wine-flavoured skirt away from the upholstery. She didn't like the tone in which Alexis had spoken.

He moved forward and threw a switch, and immediately the rush of warm air engulfed her. 'That should keep you warm until I get you home. But you really shouldn't be shivering.'

She couldn't say, 'I'm not shivering because I'm cold, but because of the way you speak sometimes.' Then she found she didn't need to answer. The big car was pulling in silently before the steps of her own house.

Stepping out carefully when her door was opened, again Clarissa gathered her skirt close. It might be ruined, but there was no need to get stains on the immaculate trousers of the man waiting there.

'Your keys, Clarissa!' he was saying. But, fumbling for them in her small evening purse, she kept them in her hand and told him,

'Look, there's no need for you to come up. The veranda light is on, and you have a garden full of guests.'

'Yes, there *is* need for me to come up. And my garden full of guests can wait. Your keys.'

Perforce she handed them over, and, treading the stairs beside him, stood well away from him while he opened the door. He didn't return the keys. He reached in to switch on the light, then stood back with a gesturing hand for her to precede him.

He put the keys on a small table, then stood back and smiled—a smile that reached across and encircled her, sending her bones melting to liquid. Alexis, she thought. Oh, Alexis, I shouldn't have come up here to where you live. Her lids fell shut.

'Clarissa!' The one word came to her in a tone she had never heard Alexis use before. Her eyes flew open, startled. He said again, 'Clarissa . . .' and his hands reached out to clasp her shoulders. As those fingers brought her closer, no thoughts now of a wine-drenched skirt touching him threaded her consciousness.

She was gazing into eyes just inches away—not eyes turning black now with anger. They had concentrated into diamond pinpoints, and as she was drawn closer and his head came down, her lids fell again with only one thought colouring her mind. This was Alexis!

The kiss he was bestowing on her was not like the one she remembered from so long ago. Oh no, that had been demanding, angry, passionate! This one was soft and gentle, his lips moving warmly upon her own. And, suddenly, she didn't care . . . all other thoughts washed away. She collapsed into him; and on tiptoe, her hands clasping behind his neck, she began returning all the warmth, the caresses, the demanding desire that he was abruptly pouring on her.

Then suddenly she was stood away, the hard fingers upon her shoulders holding her there tightly. She felt the disjointed, ragged breath he drew; she heard the sharp

expletive he uttered. Then, unexpectedly, he was smiling at
her again and saying in the soft voice he could use
sometimes, 'Until I met you, my dear Clarissa—even when
I . . .' He stopped speaking for a moment, then continued,
'I had no trouble whatsoever in doing only what I decided to
do, what I wanted to do, but now . . . Look, I seem to meet
you in the most unreal situations, and at the most unreal
times. But this time for now has got to finish and I have to
go.

'As you've said, my party needs my attention. But
first . . . just to remember me by.' His hands slid, oh, so
slowly down her bare arms and from their passage Clarissa
felt every nerve-end send its warning. The dark head bent,
overhead light catching the fairness within it, and he
dropped a kiss into the prised-open palm, before closing it
into a small fist.

He turned without another word or look, and Clarissa
heard only the decisive click of the front door as it closed
sharply behind him.

She moved backwards, knowing there was a sofa behind
her, and sank on to its arm. This was silly, she told herself,
feeling empty and shaking. What she had done those few
seconds ago was also silly, when she had responded so
completely. And once again she knew she should never have
come up to this place.

Maybe in time she would have forgotten a shadowy figure
that had coloured her growing-up years. But
now . . . Even though a product of her generation, with
television and films force-fed to it, she had still found no
romantic interest in anyone . . . any other man. So,
fatalistically now, she knew that after tonight there never
would be any other. Only Alexis!

So where did that leave her? She glanced down at the still
closed fist. He had said as he placed that small caress into it,
'Just to remember me by.' She hadn't needed that gesture to
remember him. No, of course she hadn't. Her fingers went
up to her lips, covering the place where other kisses had

lingered—scorching, passionate kisses.

What was it that Alice had said to Sarah that day in the car? 'He's out of your league, Sarah.' Well, he would also be right out of hers. Alexis was one of the largest cane-farmers around here; and listening to the casual gossip which had gone the rounds of the staff-room after they had received the invitation for tonight's barbecue, she had heard also that he had other wealth as well.

Even if he hadn't married in all these years after he had broken his engagement—and it had certainly been Alexis who had done that, not Delys—he still didn't give the appearance of being a star-crossed lover; rather the reverse, in fact, she thought, remembering how he had looked and behaved with the beautiful and assured Lesley Armitage.

She also remembered the dancing amusement those unusual slate-grey eyes had carried when her headmaster had introduced her at the school that day. He *did* remember her, but it was probably only as the young girl he had taken for a ride on his windsurfer, and had kissed so thoroughly on a dark river bank when he shouldn't have done so. Maybe that was the reason he had swung her behind the oleander trees to warn her against Fred Martinez—a small feeling of responsibility for a young girl he had once known.

But he had had no need to do that. Clarissa knew she would take up no invitations from a practised charmer like Fred Martinez. He *was* handsome, an undeniable attraction did radiate from him. But as far as she was concerned, he was shark country, and she would keep right away from him.

She unclasped her little fist, glanced down at her ruined frock and, pushing herself upright, walked shakily to the bathroom. Her lovely dress and her half slip were pulled off and went into a plastic garbage bag. It was no use trying to wash out that stain; it would always show. And she didn't want to be reminded of the way Lesley Armitage had looked so pointedly at her with that malicious amusement.

Standing under the shower, she allowed it to run for a long time, then, wrapped in a large towel, she walked along the corridor to her room. Slipping into a short cotton nightdress, she picked up her brush and began to brush her hair in long, smooth strokes.

The soothing motion brought her metabolism back to normal and, the shaking gone, she walked over to the window to look out into what someone had said was a lucky night for Alexis.

Suddenly the brush in her hand was dropped on to the dressing-table, the overhead light was switched off, and she climbed into bed. An arm thrown over closed eyes, deliberately she allowed herself to think of Alexis' kisses. She knew that being with him was all she asked of life. But life didn't give one everything one asked for; even in her short existence she had come to know that.

Still, she knew that Alexis liked kissing her, even if he had shown no sign that it was anything more than just that! At times he had shown amusement, but he had also shown that threatening demeanour she had seen tonight. He certainly hadn't behaved as a man does when beginning to start a romantic attachment . . . or a love affair.

But then, abruptly, without even meaning it to happen, she was in his arms, fused into him, body to body, feeling again those sliding coils of passion unwinding her every nerve-end. She went with no inhibition at all, returning kisses which had begun with so gentle a warmth, but which had run flaring like a scorching forest fire, demanding, desire-laden.

Her body flung sideways and she knew she would have to stop this. She wondered if she could leave this town, try for a transfer, and even as she thought it, she knew absolutely that she couldn't. Oh, well, she would just have to keep out of Alexis' way, that was all. And now she was going to sleep. She *was*!

But she heard the ticking of her bedside clock sound the hours away. She heard the others come home. She made herself try to prepare lessons in her mind, but it wasn't until the false dawn stained the horizon with a chill grey that she finally dropped into the oblivion of sleep.

CHAPTER FIVE

THE TWO girls walked out on to the school veranda. Sarah said, 'Come into town with me in Peter's car. You can help me shop.'

Clarissa laughed. 'You have to be joking,' was all she vouchsafed. 'I did my shopping last week. You should get yourself better organised, Sarah. No, I'm for the school bus.'

She put up her umbrella and hurried down the steps, still smiling. It was Sarah's week for buying the food and cooking their meals and, unlike Alice and Clarissa, who did their one big shopping on a Saturday morning, Sarah always needed things. Spoilt and looked after all her life, she got through her week's chores haphazardly, but still, she did get through them.

There were only two stops before her own came and, thanking the driver, Clarissa climbed down. Walking home as fast as she could through the drizzling rain, she opened the letterbox to collect the mail and hurried up the steps.

Dropping both the letters and her big shoulder-bag on to the small table beside the front door, she eased off her raincoat and kicked off her shoes. Then, padding out through to the kitchen, she unlocked the back door and hung her coat on a hanger. She grinned suddenly at the thought of the way Sarah would dispose of hers; probably on the floor!

Returning for her bag, Clarissa glanced through the mail, knowing there was one from her mother, having already noted the coloured envelope Mrs Raymond used. She took it and, straightening the others, stopped with a small frown between her brows. There was a second one for her.

The crease on her forehead deepened. Just looking at it sent a tingle through the nerves of every finger holding it.

44

There was no reason to be thinking what she was think-ing—in fact, she told herself, it was stupid. Yet she still stood carefully holding the heavy cream envelope, with her name and address scrawled across it in heavy black script.

She turned and marched for her own room and, dropping her shoulder-bag with her mother's letter on the edge of the bed, sat there herself, crumpling the immaculately spread quilt.

Reaching into the bag, she found a pencil, and rolling it beneath the flap she withdrew the one sheet of cream paper folded in half.

The writing began abruptly with only a name.

> Clarissa,
> I have to be away on cane business for a few weeks.
> Owing to the circumstances of our last meeting, I thought
> it might be in order to inform you of the reason for my
> absence.
>
> > Alexis.

Clarissa read it through twice, but could find nothing more in it but what the bare words said. Still—she curled up tightly on the bed—he had been right. She would have wondered, but she would also have accepted that he was living his life, and that she would have to go about living her own.

However, smiling suddenly, she wondered what were those circumstances he had in mind—the ruin of her lovely dress, or the beginnings of a torrid love scene. Oh, Alexis . . .!

She was again curled up, but in a different place this time, on the sofa in the living-room, when Sarah returned, accompanied by Alice.

Laughing, she looked them over. 'Did she co-opt you, Alice? You're both loaded down!'

'Clarissa . . .' Sarah spoke her name a little hesitantly, 'I know you don't care for it very much, but as I'm going out tonight, I've only bought Kentucky Fried for dinner. We can heat it up, and I'll make a salad . . .'

'No, you won't make her a salad. She can eat chips and coleslaw as we're going to,' Alice broke in.

Clarissa laughed again. 'OK, Alice, but you like chips and Kentucky Fried!' Then, as both girls turned round to face her, she said, 'Don't be silly—I don't mind eating with my fingers occasionally. And really, we must study poor Sarah. Only think of what a little bit of washing-up there'll be for her to do!' Clarissa ducked sharply as a cushion came hurtling her way.

They ate their dinner—with both forks and fingers. And glancing around the table, Clarissa reflected again how lucky she had been to be billeted with these two.

On Sunday three weeks later they went to the beach. Lying under a big colourful umbrella, Clarissa surveyed the scene; this place she had been to once before. There were windsurfers out on the ocean, showing brilliant sails with their vivid crimsons and yellows, their greens and orange. But on none of them flying over that blue sea out there was there a tall, bronzed figure that she knew.

She was smiling dreamily, thinking of Alexis, wondering where he was, what he was doing at this moment, remembering that precious note tucked away, when she had to throw up a hand to protect her face from flying sand as Sarah dropped down beside her.

'Had enough swimming?' she asked, and grinned widely. Yes, Sarah had had enough, because with her skin and colouring she went into the ocean for only the obligatory dip. But she enjoyed the beach in other ways, and soon it wasn't only the two girls under the big umbrella.

'Hey, Clarissa!' called Stan. 'We're going to get up a weekend trip sailing through the Hinchenbrook Channel calling in at some of the islands on the way. Oh, it won't be for a month or so, because we'd better wait until the wet season is over. But would you be in on it?'

Sidestepping an answer to the core of Stan's question, Clarissa asked, 'Do you actually mean that in around a month or so the wet season disappears, just like that?'

'Well, I'm not saying it all goes, just like that—weather and the good Lord being unpredictable. However . . .' Stan grinned round at the listening faces, 'we mostly have the wet season from November to March, give or take a little before or after. But then the climate up here is all anyone can ask for. Now, how about that weekend?'

Clarissa glanced at Alice, who had also come along to join them, but Alice shook her head, saying, 'No, we won't be going. But a weekend sailing the Channel would be just the thing for you, Clarissa, as you haven't yet done that——' She paused for a moment, and gazed at Stan before continuing, 'Always providing, of course, that you go with a reliable skipper, and in a reliable boat.'

'Oh, come on, Alice! Eddie, why don't you keep her under control?' asked Stan of his fellow worker, but at receiving only a laughing gesture of acquiescence, he continued, 'I'll have you know, anything I arrange is always reliable. Now, how about it, Clarissa?'

It was Clarissa's turn to laugh at him. 'I'll have to think about it, but now I'm going for a swim.'

Rising, she ran across the hard white sand, wondering why she hadn't accepted. It would probably be a great weekend with that sort of crowd, and she knew fatalistically that she mightn't accept when, or if, the expedition did eventuate.

Then at the water's edge, she shook her head. She knew why she hadn't accepted at once, and she thought again, as she had done countless times, that she couldn't keep on running her life with a shadowed presence always on the outskirts of it. She shrugged and took a running dive into the creaming waves.

But it was only the next day that Alice, normally the last home, but early today, greeted her with, 'There's a large parcel on the table for you, Clarissa. Mrs Peel signed for it.' Mrs Peel was their next-door neighbour.

'For me? I'm not expecting a parcel.' Puzzlement

sounded in Clarissa's voice. Then she added, 'I expect it could be from my mother. She's the only person I'd be receiving parcels from.' She walked over to the dining-room table and gazed down at a large, flat box.

No tingling nerve-ends this time at receiving unexpected mail. A label, typewritten with her name and address, was all that met her gaze. A furrow came between her eyes. It didn't look like a parcel her mother would send. Still . . .

'Open it, why don't you?' interrupted Sarah, who was standing beside her. 'If it was me, I'd have had the paper ripped off by this time!'

Clarissa turned from the package for a brief moment to smile at her. 'OK, I'm going to now. I just can't think who it could be from, though.' So, tearing off the wrappings, she disclosed a large dress box. And somewhere deep inside her, without any will of her own setting it in motion, a pulse leaped. She knew abruptly, without any second of doubt, what this box contained.

She eased off the lid and moved aside tissue paper. A glint of yellow, absolute golden yellow, met her gaze, with a plain white card resting between its vivid folds.

Without reading, she knew who had penned those few sprawling words in stark black script. They said,

With apologies,

Alexis.

'Oh, Clarissa!' Alice had come over too to pause beside them. 'It's because your other frock was ruined at his barbecue. How like Alexis!'

Only the three words were there. Anyone could read them and accept them only for what they said. An apology.

'Never mind the silly card. Take out the dress and let's all see it.' Sarah's attitude, as always, came down to basics.

Shaken out, the frock was a creation in sun-yellow heavy linen, straight and loose from the shoulders to just above the knees, where it then descended to calf-length in a myriad tiny pleats. It was Clarissa's size. And it was lovely.

Alice exclaimed, 'Oh, it's lovely!'

'Yes,' was all Clarissa replied, and added, 'But there was no need for him to send it.'

'Of course there was,' said Sarah. 'That dress of yours which was ruined was a lovely one too; this just makes up for it.'

'I'll put it away.' Clarissa gathered up tissue paper and wrappings and walked down the corridor. Alice began setting the table for their meal. Sarah went to the telephone to begin phoning.

In the privacy of her room, without any more ado, Clarissa hung the dress away, right at the back of her wardrobe. She didn't know how she felt about it. She had known immediately how she felt about his letter. 'All right, coming!' she answered Alice's call for dinner.

But it was four days later on a Friday evening that what had started out as a comedy of errors turned into something very different. Clarissa was going out of the school gate when the deputy head ran after her. 'Look,' he said, 'can you do us a favour, Clarissa?'

'Of course, Peter, if I can. What do you need?'

'I was going over to town to coach the debating team, but that clot Stevens has gone and got himself hurt at football, so I have to follow the ambulance to the hospital. You did a bit of debating in Brisbane, didn't you?'

'Yes, I debated, but I didn't coach.'

'But you can take over until I come. It's only primary school stuff. Look, Mrs Green will drop you at the hall. If I don't turn up by the time you've finished, ring the boss to come and get you, OK? I must be off.'

Clarissa sighed, then went over to where Mrs Green's car was parked. In front of the hall both teams, their own, and the other youngsters, were waiting, complete with parents.

The time passed, and smugly Clarissa thought she had managed quite credibly. And at the finish when they all began departing and closing up the hall she went with them and waited outside. She wondered if Peter was still at the hospital, then, as the minutes lengthened, she hesitated, not knowing what to do.

Still, she couldn't keep on waiting here; it would be dark soon, because this far north twilight was non-existent. It was daylight one minute, dark the next.

So she began walking. Too bad if Peter missed her. He could check at her home later, and she certainly wasn't going to ring the headmaster. She'd go over to East Ingham, which was on her way, and get a cab from the taxi-rank there. She would probably need to, she decided, glancing up at the lowering grey sky. It would certainly begin to rain soon.

She was quite happy to be walking, pleasantly and in no hurry. This was one of the nicest country towns she had been in, sparkling clean with wide streets, and completely law-abiding.

Passing over the bridge, she walked through East Ingham, but saw no taxis. Then, half-way to home, the rain came down. So, hoisting her large shoulder-bag higher, Clarissa raised her face to the streaming downpour. If you had to be out in this kind of rain, that was better than trudging along, hunched up.

A few cars passed, but it wasn't until she was nearly home that one went by, then came to an abrupt halt with suddenly applied brakes.

'Damn,' she muttered. 'Whoever it is, I wish they'd go on their way. I'm too wet to get into any car.'

A door was opened beside her and a voice said, 'Get in!'

'I'm nearly home, Alexis. I'm wet through. I'll just go on.'

'Get in!'

As she still stood, hesitating, the rain pouring down on her, the voice from inside the big car said, 'If I have to, I'll come out and get you, then we'll both be drenched.'

He would too, she knew. So she stepped in gingerly, curling up in the seat as close to the door as she could get. She said, 'I didn't know you were home again.'

'I got back yesterday. What in the name of heaven are you doing wandering around in the rain like this?'

Wearily she replied, 'It's too long a story. Look, here we are.'

Alexis had pulled to a stop in front of their house—a house in complete darkness.

'There's no light. Where are the others?' he asked, and as she went to open the door, he gestured to her, then threw a switch on the dashboard.

'Where are the others?' he asked again.

Violently angry that this had happened, that Alexis had come along at this one time to see her like this, sopping wet, hair hanging in rats' tails, Clarissa answered only because she knew she would have to.

So she said curtly, only wanting to be out of the car, and out of her drenched clothes, 'Sarah's gone home for the weekend. Alice and Eddie have gone up to Cairns to see about a new job at the hospital there—promotion or something for him.'

Again Clarissa went to open the door. It wouldn't budge. 'I'd like to get out, Alexis,' she said. 'I'm getting cold.'

The car was started, and wet gravel spurted beneath the wheels. She sat up straight. 'What are you doing? Where are you going, Alexis?'

'I'm taking you home—to my home. But there's no need to be alarmed—abduction and rape aren't on the agenda. As you said, you're sopping wet. You'd go into that empty house, and I expect no doubt have a bath, but would you bother to prepare a decent meal? Now, at my place everything is laid on.'

Angrily she snapped, 'You're being silly, Alexis! Good heavens, I'm twenty-two years old . . . and I've looked after myself for . . .' She stopped. She really hadn't looked after herself for long. But she hadn't been a pampered young girl, either. Of course she could look after herself.

Receiving no answer, she glared across at him. He was watching the road, gazing with slitted eyes at the blazing lights reaching out to them through the streaming rain. Then they were off the main road and on to his private track.

He didn't bring the big car to a halt at the front steps, but drove around the side. There *was* a light at his place giving outline to all the barbecue area.

Clarissa stepped from the car—what else could she do—and with fingers, lightly this time, guiding her, walked through this familiar place to the back door.

However, the room she entered wasn't familiar, and all she was aware of was reflected brightness—from tiles, from benches, from gleaming fittings. It was only an impression she received, because she was hurried through into a corridor running the length of the house. Those light fingers on her elbow directed her to the right, and in just a few yards Alexis opened a door. He said, 'This bathroom isn't mine; it's a guest bathroom,' and, walking inside, pushed open sliding glass doors and turned on taps.

Then passing her as he returned to the door, he told her curtly, 'Get undressed and hand your clothes out to me to be put in the dryer. Then get under that hot shower, Clarissa.' The door closed with a snap.

Clarissa leaned back against the wall. Everything had happened too quickly. Then, hearing the scrape of a step outside, she began swiftly to undress. As she took off her wet skirt and blouse, an almost hysterical giggle escaped her. As far as this house and its owner were concerned, she must be accident-prone. If they could think, her clothes must be imagining the same thing. This was the second time . . .

A peremptory knock came on the door, and a voice in a tone she knew said, 'If you think that giving me your clothes to dry is some big deal, Clarissa, allow me to inform you that during the long years of my life such garments have not been unfamiliar to me. Now hurry up!'

No, she bet they hadn't, she thought bleakly. So, with a towel wrapped sarong-fashion about her, she bundled up skirt and blouse, pants and bra, and opening the door,

handed them through. She saw no more of Alexis than a
tanned hand receiving them.

It wasn't cold up in this climate, but she had been very
wet, and the rain had seemed cold, so she enjoyed the hot
shower she had been ordered to take. Then with a towel
wrapped turban-fashion around her wet hair, she began
towelling herself dry. Before she had time to wonder if she
was to go outside just dressed in two towels, there came a
knock and Alexis' voice said, 'I have a dressing-gown for
you, Clarissa. It will do until your clothes are dry.' The door
came open an inch or so, and a bundle of dark blue silk
slithered to the floor.

Well, when in Rome . . . she reflected, and picked it up.
The gown reached to the floor, but a tight belt would fix
that, she surmised, and she had to turn the sleeves up and
up. With lipstick applied carefully she drew a deep breath,
tied the belt firmly, and in bare feet walked out to meet
whatever the evening had in store for her.

Alexis was standing with his back to the doorway, busy
with something on a bench. Clarissa stood gazing at him,
actually taking in the way he looked tonight for the first time.
And also for the first time she didn't see him in immaculate,
fashionable hand-made gear. He was wearing casual knock-
about fawn cords, with a short-sleeved open-necked darker
brown shirt.

She had made no noise whatsoever arriving here on bare
feet, but suddenly his head turned and across the empty
space between them he looked at her. He smiled, saying,
'You look very fetching. I'm sure that dressing-gown didn't
do the things for me that it does for you!'

I bet it did a darn sight more, she thought, but said only,
'It feels very luxurious, but will my clothes be dry now?'

'I don't expect so, and anyway, we have to eat now.
Come along over here.'

CHAPTER SIX

CLARISSA moved across to a table positioned before long plate-glass windows, sat in the chair pulled out for her and noticed that two places were set, and that Alexis was returning with two bowls.

'Here, eat it up,' he told her. 'I do know the weather isn't cold, and I know that now you're dry you'll be OK, but you weren't dry, and hot soup never hurt anyone.' He began to break up a crisp roll on the plate beside him, then casually started to eat.

Clarissa knew he was there, but she drank the soup, her attention given carefully to it. Almost finished, and becoming aware of only a stillness across from her, she glanced up.

He was sitting silently, elbow on table, chin cupped in hand, looking over at her. And suddenly there was a new dimension in the atmosphere. Throughout all these unexpected happenings of tonight, no ideas of emotional involvement or of lovemaking had intruded. Alexis had behaved only as a friend who had seen another friend wet through and walking in the rain. Every single part of his attitude had been just that.

Now, in this very large, silent house, another atmosphere had intruded. She couldn't bring herself to break that gaze. But it appeared that Alexis could. He had stood up and, taking his soup bowl, walked away to the bench beside the stove.

Freed, Clarissa looked down. There wasn't a lot of soup left, and she moved her spoon round and round in it.

Why? She had asked herself that question before. Why did he show this interest in her, and yet do nothing about it? She was sure that if he had come across another girl he knew, Sarah for instance, he would certainly have stopped. But he

54

would have taken her to her own home, courteously seen her inside and then said a pleasant goodnight.

Of course she was a product of today's world, and of course she knew what happened in it. Alexis *did* like to kiss her, she acknowledged that. But still, with all he had going for him, he could obtain all the feminine company he would need, to kiss . . . or whatever.

So why . . .? Why go to the trouble he did about her? Again she asked herself if it could be because he had once kissed a schoolgirl—and in the way that he had done so long ago.

No, it wasn't that! Although that episode might have made their relationship a little more than just meeting a casual newcomer, did he . . .? Her hand clenched on the spoon she was holding, then just as suddenly she forced it to relax. Did he want just an affair and was setting about his own way of arranging it?

She knew absolutely that though the only thing in the world she really wanted was to belong to Alexis, she didn't want to be just an affair to him for a few months. To have him go then on his way . . . no, of course she didn't.

Here a wry smile twisted her mouth as she remembered she had thought that Alexis didn't give the impression of being a star-crossed lover; because she certainly was. But even if she was, she wasn't going to give that impression either.

A hand came within her downcast vision, the bowl was whisked away and a plate with two crumbed slices of fish was set in its place. 'I might not be the best fryer of fish,' said Alexis' voice from beside her, 'but I am considered a very good hand as a maker of salads.'

These words did bring her glance up. He was smiling at her, a nice ordinary smile, and everything was back to normal again. Answering, she told him, 'I can cook, but I'm afraid it's only plain cooking. My mother thought I should know how.'

'Do you know, Clarissa, it seems so strange to me at this moment, but I find I don't know anything about you. About the actual you, I mean. The things you like, what you do . . .' Alexis paused for a moment, and that brilliant amused smile she had witnessed before shone out as he continued, 'except, of course, that you seem to like windsurfing!'

All through this strange evening Clarissa hadn't blushed or been embarrassed at all, not even when handing out to him every stitch she wore, but now suddenly, gazing across at him, she felt the hot colour stain her cheeks. Yes, she had liked windsurfing—and the man who had taken her for a ride on one.

Alexis smiled across at her and unexpectedly she was smiling back, and with him began to eat her dinner. She knew she was eating the fish; she knew she was picking up pieces of salad from the separate bowl by her plate, but she also knew she wouldn't be able to remember the particular taste of either.

'So,' said her companion after a few minutes of only eating, 'tell me about yourself.'

A small frown forming on her forehead, Clarissa didn't know how to reply for a few moments. It seemed a strange request. 'There's really nothing to tell, Alexis,' she said. 'I'm just an ordinary girl leading an ordinary life.'

'Oh, I wouldn't expect that to be the case. Not when you look at a man from under those long lashes, and in that certain way . . . I would imagine your existence would be far from ordinary.'

Astounded, she gazed across at him. She had blue eyes, nice eyes certainly, but they were not a spectacular sapphire or cornflower blue, and yes, her lashes were long, but they were fair and not at first noticeable.

So it was with astringency that she replied, 'Really, Alexis, don't be silly! If we're to talk about eyes, just look at your own. *They* catch the attention immediately one meets you.'

She hadn't been thinking of what she was saying, just replying to his own remarks, so it was with astonishment that she thought she saw a tinge of red colour the handsome countenance opposite—and was glad. He had done that to her often enough.

'We weren't talking about me. You were the subject. You mentioned a mother, and I think I met her when you were up here visiting the Smiths. Any other relations?'

'No. My father died when I was eleven. Nothing spectacular like a plane or car crash. It was just after a short illness, and my mother, though she was attractive, never seemed interested in anyone else. She was a very self-contained person.' Here Clarissa laughed softly before continuing. 'I think she was only waiting for me to grow up and get settled. She disliked the city, and in my last year of college she put our small house on the market, sold it, saw me into a hostel for my last few months and then flew to Darwin.'

'Didn't you mind?'

'Mind?' Puzzlement coloured Clarissa's query. Then she laughed. 'No, of course I didn't mind. We have a good relationship, my mother and I. I can't remember her ever hugging or kissing me as I've seen happen between other girls and their mothers. But she was always there when I needed her, and, as I told Sarah, she did keep me one of the best-dressed girls at school. No, of course I didn't mind! I only hope she loves Darwin, because she certainly didn't like Brisbane.'

Alexis shook his head as if puzzled at something in his turn, then glanced up sharply as she asked casually, 'And what about the story of *your* life?'

'Oh no, you don't,' he answered. 'And besides, you do know some of it, and you can hear the rest another time. Do you drink tea or coffee?' The last sentence closed the previous subject with finality.

And Clarissa recognised that it was so as she watched Alexis busying himself once more at a bench, making the tea she had opted for.

Drinking it idly, she asked, 'Do you work all the year, Alexis? Jerry said something about cane being only a six-month job.'

· 'Did he really? I'll have to put him on a farm! But yes, I
expect if you didn't want to keep your farm in A1 condition, if
you didn't care if your fields weren't ploughed and rested
properly, didn't check that your new crop was planted when it
should be planted, and didn't do the thousand and one things
that are needed to have a successful cane harvest—yes, you
could manage with working only half a year—but not on my
farm!

'Still,' he continued, 'one does begin cutting in June, when
the mills start crushing, and that crushing does finish in
December. So most farmers take their holidays around March
or April when they've cleaned up their fields and got the new
plantings under way. I do!'

'It's almost the end of April now. Are you going away, or
did you make the sugar conference a holiday?' Clarissa smiled
over at him, only speaking casually.

He didn't reply for more than a minute, so she made
herself break the small silence. 'I expect you like cane-
farming?'

'I expect I do.' Alexis' teeth gleamed suddenly in the bright
overhead light as he smiled. 'I've never thought about it, but
as it's the only thing I've ever done, and I like my life, I
suppose I do like farming.'

Glancing down, he picked up his cup to finish his tea, and
her gaze roved over the downbent head, wishing she could
reach out and smooth back the hair, still damp from the rain,
which was falling across his forehead.

Then unexpectedly his gaze had risen. She hadn't been
expecting it, and as their eyes met, and held, the teacup in her
own hand remained motionless.

Alexis' glance shifted, and his chair went skittering over the
polished tiled floor as it was pushed sharply back. He said,
'We'll get your clothes.'

Clarissa looked down at the table, at the clutter of used
dishes, and began gathering them together. Alexis said curtly,
'Leave them!'

So, rising, she went before him as he indicated, and in the

doorway, endeavouring to pass him without going too close, she tripped on the long gown. Her arm outflung for balance wasn't enough, and she was falling. Another arm, tanned, corded muscles rigid, gripped her.

Violently angry with herself, she thought furiously that tripping, getting caught up like this, could have seemed a deliberate action. But she hadn't been able to help it; the silk dressing-gown had slipped from the tied belt and hung lopsided. She went to disengage herself, fierce anger at what had happened overriding all else. Then she glanced quickly at Alexis. He was looking down at her, down at the silken covering which was spread and gaping now, exposing almost the whole top half of her body.

Abruptly, two arms were upon her, one going low upon her back, spreadeagling, bringing her to him, the other, lying against her throat, sending fingers caressing softly back and forth.

Her breath caught, and at her involuntary movement of withdrawal, the arm around her tightened . . . tightened to bring them more closely together, fused into one entity. Then that handsome head bent, not to set his lips to hers but to let them trail down across her jawline, along the thrown-back exposed throat, and then on . . . and on . . .

Clarissa knew that from somewhere deep inside, her whole body had shuddered when those lips stopped. Stopped to rest between the fine line cleaving her breasts before they began to move again, slowly, and oh, so softly, sideways. Her eyes closed, and she found that she had gone in the space of seconds beyond thought, beyond coherence, beyond everything except a driving need, which was as clear to her as though written in letters of fire across the dimness of this silent corridor.

For a moment, an aeon, she responded to Alexis' demands, as their two figures stood enclosed together in the big, empty, silent house. Then it was the man's body which contracted with a ripple that spread completely through it. But Clarissa only moved closer, her head thrown back, fair hair cascading over the bronzed arm supporting it.

She couldn't see those eyes, concentrated to brilliant pinpoints now as he gazed down at her; gazed at the form, the body, open and exposed entirely to him—his for the taking. She didn't see him bend, his lips coming down at last to rest on her own . . . and then stop. Nor that for a brief second he stood there motionless as if some unwelcome thought had intruded.

Then she was pushed away, her back resting against the hard wall behind her, two arms extending on either side, making her a prisoner. Her eyes came open, and she saw him only inches away—but the tension emanating from the big solid body so close held her captive as if still in his arms.

'Clarissa . . .' Her name came slurred. Then came also a deep indrawn breath. Alexis said, and the words reached right into the depths of her being, 'More than anything I want to take you and make love to you . . . but you're so young, and . . .'

'I'm not young. I'm twenty-two!' Clarissa knew she said the words, but the tone in which she said them was not her own either.

Then was there a hint of lightness breaking through that note of heavy passion which coloured his whole demeanour? However, he only said, 'Yes, and that is young. I've just had my thirty-first birthday, and my twentieth is so far distant, it seems lost in the cradle of time.

'And speaking of youth, maybe it's what happened all those years ago that's the cause of this thin invisible line which seems to stretch between us. Because there is an empathy. And I have to be more careful with you because of the shocking way I behaved to a very young schoolgirl.'

Clarissa went to shake her head, but her companion was continuing, 'I did go over to the Smiths' to see you the morning after I met you on the river bank. But you'd already left.'

Again she went to shake her head, then made herself speak. 'It didn't matter. I knew at the time you were angry.'

'Yes, I was angry, but that was no excuse!' Alexis was quiet for some little time, and she couldn't bring herself to break the silence about them.

Then, 'Clarissa . . .' he began, and stopped once more, before going on, 'Have you ever been in love? Have you ever loved anyone?'

The words hung in a silence that brought her upright against the hard wood at her back, and her head swung away from the eyes watching her from so short a distance.

What was she to answer? She couldn't bring herself to say no, I haven't, to either of those questions. If she said yes, I have, he would think it was some man in Brisbane, and she really couldn't allow that.

She said, 'You ask the strangest questions, Alexis, at the strangest times. I don't think I have to answer.'

The reply that came carried no sign of tense emotion this time. The words echoed flatly. 'You did understand what I meant by that second question?'

Oh, she had understood all right. This was the eighties they were living in. Of course she had understood! And in ordinary circumstances it would be no business of his.

But what answer could she give him? She couldn't lie to Alexis. A lie was a thing he would never forgive. So she said, 'Accepting your meaning to that last question—no, I haven't loved anyone. Now, I want to go and get my clothes.' Damn him, she thought. He had no right to put her in such a position!

A hand reached out, and the backs of his fingers trailed down her cheek to her throat. But, involuntarily her arm went out to halt it. Then the imprisoning arms had dropped and, walking before her, Alexis had turned into a room which she saw was a laundry.

He opened the lid of a machine and brought out two scraps of lace and nylon, then shook out the thin lawn blouse. Reaching in again, he brought out, and went to shake also, the fawny-brown skirt.

Clarissa closed her eyes, but opened them again at once.

The skirt was a complete mess. As it was such a good one, she had always only hand-washed and drip-dried it. Her glance meeting that of Alexis, she said, keeping her voice smooth and the expression in her eyes as hidden as she could manage, 'That's all right; it'll iron out. I'll just take them and go and get dressed.' She reached out a hand to gather up all the garments.

But Alexis had turned away. He swung out an ironing-board from its wall position and switched on a gleaming ivory and chrome iron.

'Show me,' he said. 'Because you're not going home for anyone to see you dressed in that. And really, Clarissa, you might think you can tell lies, but don't ever imagine you can tell them to me.'

Angrily she gazed across at him, at that tall figure lounging now so indolently against the far wall. Her voice cold, she replied, 'You can think what you like to think! I can do what I have to do, or what I want to do!'

Bringing her attention completely from him, she checked that the iron was on steam, and eased the skirt over the board. 'Please,' she prayed softly, 'please let the thing iron out—even to be just presentable!' But gazing down at it, she wondered. Then a blinding thought struck at her and she raised her glance swiftly.

Alexis was looking at the outspread shirt, his eyes half shut, hooded. Clarissa spoke sharply into the silence. 'Don't you dare!'

The hooded eyes instantly came wide open, their gaze directed completely across at her, and they were filled with a glinting, laughing brilliance. Alexis said softly, 'Don't I dare what, Clarissa?'

'Don't you dare send me a skirt. This one was old and ready for the scrap-bag anyway.' She told the outrageous lie without the least quiver in her firm tone, pushing away the knowledge that this skirt had been another of her mother's acquisitions.

She began to run the warm iron over the skirt. It didn't

make much impression, so, turning up the steam indicator to its outer edge, she pressed harder, and saw thankfully that the material *was* straightening out, when a soft voice said, 'Do you have things sent to you, then, Clarissa?'

Blankly she looked at him, wondering what he could be on about; thinking that at least he could also straighten up, and not lounge there in that position as if he owned the earth. Then abruptly a hand flew up to her mouth.

'Oh, heavens—yes! I'm sorry! I'm sorry I haven't said thank you for my beautiful dress.' Then, her tone going curt, she continued, 'But how could I have? This is the first time I've seen you since I received it, and tonight hasn't been one of those normal social occasions, has it?' She wasn't smiling; but if anything, her companion's silent laughter grew deeper.

'And did you like the dress?'

'Of course I did. You knew I would! It's the most exquisite dress I've ever seen. You must know that. However . . .' Clarissa paused for a moment, the iron upraised in her hand. 'However,' she repeated, 'I don't know where I can wear it.'

She thought again of the exquisite sun-yellow creation. It wasn't a dress you could wear for any old occasion.

'Oh, there are plenty of places to wear dresses. Parties, lunches, church . . .'

'Yes, I can just imagine myself waltzing into church in that!' she answered, thinking that normally she wore cool cotton up here, while down south she mostly wore jeans or trousers.

'But there are different days for wearing different clothes. For instance, Easter Day or Christmas Day.'

She supposed that was true. But she wanted to get off the subject. She said, 'Anyway, thank you for it, Alexis. It's truly lovely. Now look, this is all ironed out, see?'

It was all ironed out, too. It had taken three times of ironing all round, but it looked presentable. Switching off the power, she gathered up the rest of her clothes, saying, 'Is it all right to go back to the bathroom and change?'

The lounging figure came upright from the wall. Alexis

said, still remaining at a distance, 'Yes, I think that would be the best idea.'

Clarissa couldn't read the strange nuance his tone carried.

CHAPTER SEVEN

THE SUN had been up for some few hours, but its shafts of brightness were still reaching out horizontally. One decided to sweep through an open screened window, there to play hide-and-seek over a carpet, then in and among furniture, to come at last to rest across a sleeping face. It stayed there a moment, warm, tantalising, until an arm came up as if to ward away an irritant.

Then, as if becoming aware of the brilliant intruder, long fair lashes swept upwards, and opened blue eyes glanced around. Remembrance came suddenly of last night and its happenings, and Clarissa was abruptly awake. Looking at her watch, she saw it showed after nine o'clock. I've slept in, she thought. But it had been late when she had finally got to sleep.

Going over what had happened yesterday evening, Clarissa thought yet again that she would never understand Alexis. At his barbecue, he could easily have just apologised, then called Jerry or Eddie to take her home. And, Alexis being Alexis, she could also understand him replacing her dress—but there was no need for *such* a dress.

And last night . . . suddenly she felt his body, his kisses, through every part of her. He had wanted her, and those words, those unforgettable words he had used in saying, 'More than anything I want to take you and make love to you,' seemed now to echo about her bedroom. And, given her response to him, she wondered why he hadn't gone on from there!

Because he wasn't to know that, for her, he was the only man she would ever want to make love to her. That without him, she would have to find a serious occupation to fill her life . . . Oh, well—she gave a long sigh and swung her legs

65

off the side of the bed, then with a thin housecoat over her short nightdress she wended her way out to the kitchen.

Switching on the kettle and putting bread in the toaster, Clarissa cut up paw-paw and squeezed passion fruit over it. Then carrying her breakfast tray, she walked out on to the back veranda and set it down on the slabbed barbecue table. Leaning back in her chair, she ate her fruit slowly and gazed out over the back yard.

It couldn't really be called a garden, although it had a thick velvety green lawn, as did most gardens up in this country with its prolific rainfall. It also had a hedge of hibiscus along its back fence which provided them with large, vividly coloured blooms for their dinner-table. A space in it also provided them with a quick exit to a small all-purpose shop when they didn't want to go the long front way around.

Pouring tea, she drank it and ate her toast and honey, making her mind a blank as she allowed the deep blue unclouded arch above and the green emerald of the lawn to colour her mood. Sipping her second cup of tea, at peace with the world for the time being, she jumped, literally, when the phone shrilled inside. She allowed it to ring for a minute or so, thinking it was probably for Sarah, but as it went on and on, she rose to go inside to answer it.

'Hello, Clarissa speaking,' she said into the receiver.

'I expected it would be,' came the unexpected voice replying.

Clarissa remained silent, then, taking a deep breath, she said, 'Hello Alexis.'

All she received in answer was a low, amused laugh before he spoke again. 'Seeing as you're on your own, Clarissa, I wondered if you'd care to have dinner with me?' A pause came before he added, 'At that big hotel in East Ingham—not here.'

All kinds of thoughts went running through her mind. Thoughts like, wouldn't it be foolish to go? Wouldn't it be better if she kept a distance between them? She heard her voice saying without realising it was speaking, 'Yes, thank you, I would like that, Alexis.'

'I'll call for you at seven, then. OK?'

'Yes, seven o'clock.' The receiver at the other end of the line was already laid at rest before she placed her own very gently back.

What would she wear? was her first thought, then, remembering that it was Saturday, a night for dressing up more than one usually did, she knew without more ado what she would be wearing.

The day passed, doing her hand-washing, cleaning up her room, and then, still feeling restless, she got out the bottle of polish and polished every piece of furniture in the lounge and dining-room.

Then, with her hair shampooed and blow-dried, she settled down for the last couple of hours with a book, one that she had been wanting to read and which would surely keep her interest. It didn't!

But finally the time arrived for bathing and dressing. And when she was ready, she examined herself in the mirror. Yes, she decided, as she had done the night of the barbecue, dressed and made up, she would do. She certainly wouldn't measure up to Delys, but as for Lesley Armitage . . . well?

With five minutes to seven showing on her wristwatch, she went around switching off lights except for the lounge and veranda ones, and even before finishing, she heard the soft purr of the Jaguar arriving. Opening the front door, she withdrew a few steps to pick up her small evening purse from the small doorside table.

There was the sound of footsteps running up the stairs, and Alexis was standing in the aperture. He didn't speak for a moment, just allowed his gaze to rove over her. Then he gave a low chuckle and said, 'Parade round for me.'

'No, I won't,' was the reply he received.

He walked the few steps between them and reached for her hand, turning her round himself. The golden-yellow dress swung about her knees, and Alexis said, 'I picked very well, didn't I? You look beautiful.'

Across the separating yards Clarissa looked him over in her turn. She couldn't say, as he had done, that he looked beautiful. For whatever she might look like, he looked as if he had just stepped from a high-grade fashion magazine. He wore a short-sleeved coat-shirt of startling cream which fell outside slacks of the same eye-catching pristine colour; and taking in his image as he gazed smilingly down at her, for a brief second, Clarissa's eyes closed.

It wasn't fair, she decided, then forced open her eyes to their fullest extent, making herself return his smile; making herself also find things to say that were definitely not the things she was thinking.

'Yes, I can just imagine you choosing it—going into a shop and looking round at dresses.'

'Who said anything about looking round in a shop? I go to a salon where I'm known, let me tell you, and have someone bring them to me. And I didn't need to agonise over what I selected, either. I saw that . . .' the fingers which weren't holding her hand flicked at the yellow dress, 'and I knew immediately it was the one I wanted. Was it the one you wanted too, Clarissa?'

'You know you don't need to ask. You should also know you had no need to replace my dress.'

'Oh, yes, I did! So now we'll go and dine and I can look over the table at you and admire my choice.'

Alexis drew her forward to go before him to the door and she heard it close behind him with a decisive click. Both lights, lounge and veranda, were left on. Because of course, Clarissa thought astringently, *he* wouldn't have to bother about electricity bills!

She was handed into what was now becoming a familiar seat on the passenger side of the Jaguar. She sat quietly for the short journey, and suddenly finding herself doing what she had never before until last night, realised that she did, she stopped herself quickly. Stopped looking at Alexis from under downcast lashes.

Outside the car, her arm was taken and she was piloted through a large foyer towards a dining-room, to be met there by an elderly waiter who said, 'It's good to see you here again so soon, Mr Markham. Will you be going into the bar for a pre-dinner drink, or . . .?'

Glancing down at his companion, Alexis shook his head, then told him, 'No, I think we'll just go and have our drink at the table.'

'Certainly.' The waiter went before them, between white stiffly-starched clothed and silver-laden tables, leading them to one situated a little apart from others with a wall of greenery along one side. He pulled out Clarissa's chair, then, beckoning to a younger man, smiled at Alexis and left them.

'Do you drink wine, Clarissa?' he asked her.

'I've had it occasionally. However, beer was the drink of the crowd I mixed with in Brisbane. We were all poor students, you know.'

Alexis laughed. 'OK then, I think that as we're in an Italian restaurant, and you're . . .' he stopped for a moment and looked across at her, 'still so young, we'll have . . .' he turned to the wine waiter, saying, 'a bottle of Asti Spumante, I think. Very cold!' He nodded and handed back the large wine list, returning his attention to her.

'What do you like to eat, Clarissa?' he asked, as he had enquired if she drank wine.

'That's an easy one. I like mostly all foods, but I suppose seafood is my favourite.'

'I'm afraid seafood wouldn't be the best meal to order here, but their Italian dishes are suitable for the finest gourmet. They're . . .' Alexis broke off to drink from the glass he was being offered, nodded, and watched while both their glasses were filled.

'Try it,' he told her, and raised his own glass.

Clarissa sipped carefully, then took another drink, and sent a radiant smile across to her companion. 'It's delicious!' she exclaimed. 'So cold . . . and tingly. I like it very much.'

Again she smiled widely, saying, 'I realise I don't know much about wine, but I do like this.'

'I'm glad!' Alexis leaned across and clinked his glass against the one she was holding, his eyes concentrated into those diamond pinpoints as they sometimes did when he was amused.

This is what happiness is made of, thought Clarissa. To be with him, to be in his company, doing whatever he asks. She buried her face quickly over her glass and drank.

'Would you care to go through the menu,' asked Alexis, 'or would you just like to sit and be surprised at whatever they set before you?'

'I'd love to be surprised,' answered Clarissa, and sat listening as Alexis ordered whatever he was ordering, speaking in Italian with the waiter.

She would always remember the next two hours as a present given to her out of time; a time of demarcation between the unhappy period that was to follow. They ate the delicious dishes spread before them. They talked—on ordinary subjects which held their interest. They were also interrupted occasionally by other diners, pausing on their way to speak to Alexis. And with a wry smile Clarissa was beginning to realise the reason for what she had thought was strange in the way her companion had planned their seating. Not quite, but almost, Alexis had chosen a chair which had its back to the big room.

He did answer each and every greeting in that pleasant, cool, impersonal tone of his, but then he turned back to give his entire attention to Clarissa. However, it was different with the last couple who stopped at their table, with the male half of it saying, 'Why, hello, Alexis my boy! I didn't expect to see you again so soon.'

Alexis had risen, and he was replying, 'No, but then I didn't expect to be here tonight. Allow me to present a newcomer to the district. Clarissa Raymond—Mrs Thornton, and Dr Thornton who as the hospital superintendent looks after all our health here.'

Clarissa gave the man a smile as genuine as the one this elderly, portly man was bending upon her, telling him in return for his greeting that she was happy to meet him too.

Her wide, happy smile turned into something else entirely, as she made to greet the woman. She found she was being looked over assessingly, then that the gaze from this elegant woman, much younger than her husband, was being switched to Alexis. It went over him as it had roved over Clarissa, before returning once again to the girl.

There was no prize for guessing what she was thinking and Clarissa's own expression changed. Mrs Thornton suddenly found she had a look being directed at her that was just as knowledgeable as her own had been. But Clarissa said only, 'Mrs Thornton!'

The newcomer also found that that gaze going over her, then over her husband, then over Alexis, held as much comprehension as the one she herself had used. Her glance sharpened as she took in the bland, assured face of this young girl, before she allowed her arm to be taken as Dr Thornton turned to go.

However, he was saying over his shoulder, 'How about joining us, Alexis?' But he only received a regretful shrug as the tall man facing him replied, 'I'm afraid not tonight, sir. We're just having a quick meal, as we have to eat and run.'

'Oh, well, in that case . . .' A smiling goodnight encircled them both. But as Alexis turned to glance down at her, Clarissa caught the glint in those dark grey eyes; the gleam she had come to know by now which denoted that hidden brilliance of amusement.

Once more sitting across from her, his head abruptly went down, and, puzzled, Clarissa looked across at the doubled-up figure. She saw then with astonishment that he was laughing. That it was deep, silent laughter that was causing the almost invisible shaking of those heavy, broad shoulders.

So it was with more than a tinge of sharpness that she demanded, 'And what's all that merriment in aid of?'

'It's in aid of you!' Alexis was upright again, laughter

gone, but a deep amusement still colouring his whole countenance.

'You know, Clarissa,' he continued, 'I expect it's the memory of you as a young girl which still colours my thinking of you. Mrs Thornton is regarded in some quarters as a holy terror, but she didn't faze you in the least. In fact, if I were arbitrating I'd have said you won on points. I'm beginning to wonder where all that experienced know-how comes from!'

'Oh, for heaven's sake, Alexis! I spent three years at college, being lectured by all sorts of lecturers, male and female. You get nice, kind ones; you also get the other sort, both men and women. And my mother was a great help, telling me stories about the women she served. Of course I could meet that doctor's wife on her own terms.

'And of course I knew what she was thinking while she looked us both over. Probably wishing she was here in my place, I expect,' finished Clarissa astringently.

'*Clarissa!*' Her name came out with incredulity, and the face opposite had taken on another expression. But then suddenly Alexis had swung round to allow his gaze to follow the departing couple.

'Good heavens!' was all he said, then waved to a hovering waiter to remove their plates and bring the next course.

He remained silent, and so did she, for a few minutes after fresh dishes were set before them, Clarissa furious with herself for actually saying what she had been thinking—even if what she had thought had been true. She *had* seen that expression in those eyes as they had roved over Alexis.

However, she did glance up quickly when Alexis' silence was broken as he muttered, 'Lord, it's like Old Home Week here tonight!'

Her glance, going quickly beyond him, saw Lesley Armitage and Fred Martinez moving past, and also saw thankfully that they *were* going past—to the table at the far end of the room to join the Thorntons.

There was no more mention of other diners. And her companion put himself out to be so charming that she thought disconsolately she only wished she could take this attitude of his at face value.

Finally she told him, as coffee was placed before them, cream floating on top of hers, black for Alexis, 'I wouldn't believe I could eat so much. It's been a wonderful dinner, thank you, Alexis. I'd probably only have had a salad or a sandwich at home, in front of the TV.'

Then she felt a tinge of red colour her cheeks as in his turn Alexis looked her over. However, all he said drily was, 'You don't look as if eating too much tonight would harm you.'

But later, sipping her coffee, while her companion drank his, accompanied by the brandy he had ordered for himself, she thought dreamily that this was a lovely time of the evening. There was the clinking of silver and crockery echoing gently around the big room, the pleasant sound of talk and laughter, with soft music forming a background to it all. She held her small cup in two hands, thinking of the things that happiness was made of.

Coffee and brandy finished, Alexis raised a hand, signed the bill presented to him, took a green note from a pocket, and told the waiter as he handed it over, 'Thank you. We enjoyed the dinner.'

'Thank you, Mr Markham. Come again.' The man in the red jacket went round to begin pulling out Clarissa's chair, but her companion waved him away, saying, 'I'll do that. Goodnight.'

Walking out beside him, she was glad she didn't have to pass the hospital contingent, and turned, smiling happily up at Alexis as they went through the entrance into the night. She didn't see the glance from speculative tawny eyes which followed them.

When they reached home, on the lighted veranda, Alexis held out his hand, and automatically Clarissa put her keys into it. 'I won't come in,' he told her. But he reached out to clasp both his hands behind the small of her back, bringing her into him. His kiss, when it came, however, was gentle, sweet, but as it continued the whole atmosphere changed, and her arms went up to slide behind his neck as she responded to it.

His next words came raggedly. 'I make resolutions, but my will-power is suddenly non-existent.'

Leaning far back so that she was supported by only the two hands holding her, Clarissa looked directly at him. Love, passion, acceptance, coloured his name as it echoed about them.

'Alexis!'

A breath was sharply indrawn, and she found herself stood away, the hands on her back sliding slowly from there, then over her hips and up to her shoulders. 'No, Clarissa. Tonight has ended! We'll wait for a while and see what tomorrow brings! Now . . .' One hand left her shoulder, and the backs of his fingers rested for a brief moment against her cheek. She saw the lopsided grin he gave her before she was turned and handed through the opening. He said as he closed the door upon himself, 'Lock it.'

Automatically obeying that voice, that tone, Clarissa clicked the lock and remained where she was, hearing the footsteps running down the stairs, the Jaguar's soft purr finally diminishing into silence. Then, draggingly, she flicked out both lights, and walked in the semi-darkness through to her bedroom.

She took off her lovely frock, smoothed it on a hanger and hung it away right at the back of the wardrobe. At that moment she wished she had never returned here, had never met Alexis again. Then she grinned sardonically at herself. Of course she didn't . . . no matter what the future brought, the threads of her life were entwined completely within the threads of his.

She prepared for bed, and with the clothes pulled up to her chin, she told herself, 'I'm not going to think of Alexis . . . or tonight, or, more importantly, last night, and that episode just outside his kitchen door . . . Oh no, certainly not of that!' And, surprisingly, she didn't! Almost at once, she was fathoms deep in oblivion.

CHAPTER EIGHT

WITHIN the next fortnight three things happened that connected partly one with the other. The first was seeing the thick cream envelope with the heavy black writing splashed across it waiting for her when she returned home from school. That was on Wednesday. It told her only that Alexis had been called away on cane business for ten days or so. She read it—twice—then put it carefully away in the zipped-up compartment of her handbag beside the other letter from Alexis.

Then on Sunday she was walking home from church along the footpath of the wide street when a car, a long sports car, eased slowly into the kerb beside her.

She glanced around and down, wondering. Then she saw the figure that stepped from it to hold a door open wide. 'How lucky for me to find such a charming lady to offer a lift home to! It must be my lucky day!' said Fred Martinez.

In this golden morning with not the slighest sign of rain, with a translucent arch of deep turquoise above, a heaven that showed not even the smallest cloud of puffball cotton, Clarissa smiled at him, a pleasant, friendly smile. She said, 'It's such a lovely day, Federico, I think I'll just indulge myself in strolling through it.' She showed him only smiling friendliness.

He looked back at her; this heavy, attractive man, lounging so easily by the side of the opulent-looking, low-slung maroon car. He took in the friendliness; he also took in an impression that wasn't showing. So he also smiled, while acknowledging her refusal for what it was.

'You shouldn't believe all that gossip says about me, Clarissa. I really am only offering you a lift home.'

'Oh, does gossip say things about you, Fred?' Now she

was laughing as her eyes met those tawny lion's eyes holding an expression she couldn't define. But she kept her own look friendly as she told him, 'Look, Federico—thank you for the offer, but truly, I'd rather walk home. I'm beginning to like this town very much—it's so clean and pleasant to walk through. So . . .' She sketched a half-salute with her hand, gave him another wide smile, and turned, walking away.

Her shoulders remained stiff as if waiting for someone or something to tap upon them. But the car behind remained motionless, not even starting up to drive away, and she knew that those tawny eyes were following her as she walked on.

Oh, dear! Had she done the right thing? Had she offended him when actually he had been only a pleasant acquaintance offering her a lift? But no, she hadn't been about to drive anywhere with him—and oh, yes, he had known it. Of course she wouldn't go anywhere with him! A small shiver went through her entire body when she remembered the tone a voice had carried as its owner stood behind a clump of oleander trees. When it had expressly forbidden her to have anything to do with that man back there—who was still apparently watching her.

And Alexis wouldn't have spoken so about another man without just cause, and also Jerry had . . . Impatiently, Clarissa shrugged. It *was* a lovely day, and she *was* going to enjoy her stroll home.

Then on Monday evening, as they were eating dinner, Sarah said, 'Don't forget we have to help with something for this hospital fête that the Country Women's Association is organising, to raise money for that special machine for the children's ward.'

'What fête?' Clarissa had heard nothing of it, or if she had, it had not penetrated.

'I told you some time ago, Clarissa!' said Alice a shade sharply. 'Because Eddie might not be staying on here, he wants to help make next Saturday a great success. We're all being co-opted.'

'OK,' Clarissa replied soothingly. 'Just tell me what I

have to do—or can do, and of course I'll help. Does one give things, or money, or just go and buy things.'

'It's a fête. Surely you've been to fêtes, Clarissa? They're a fact of life to raise money.'

'Of course I've heard of fêtes, and I've been to them. All through my childhood I helped when the church ran them. I say again, just tell me what I have to do.'

She was soon told what she had to do, and there was plenty of it. The Home Science mistress at the high school had also co-opted helpers for such a worthy charity. And both Alice and Clarissa—and Sarah when she could find the time—found themselves doing embroidery.

The tiny dresses, the equally small boys' suits were sewn, then given round to have the finishing touches applied. Clarissa found herself fancy-working flowers on little pockets edged with broderie anglaise, butterflies and chickens on collars edged with the same material.

And on Friday evening she shook out the small navy-blue suit to scrutinise the blue anchors she had just finished working on the square white sailor collar. She had already done a larger one on the pocket of the shorts. 'Thank goodness!' she exclaimed to Alice. 'That's the lot. And we've done a good job with all those little extra touches. They make the garments so different from off-the-peg clothes—even if I do say it myself.'

'Yes.' Complacency echoed in Alice's reply. 'How about that dress, Sarah? Is it finished?'

'It is finished, and thank the lord for that! You know how I hate sewing.'

'We do know. We've been informed more than a few times of that. But still, you've done your bit. But how in the name of goodness you're going to help Mrs Grady, I just don't know.'

'Ah!' Sarah jumped up, exclaiming gleefully, 'Just wait and I'll show you my costume.' She was off in a flash.

Alice shook her head. 'I don't know what's going to happen about that stall. It's illegal to tell fortunes for money, you know.'

Clarissa only smiled. 'That's probably right, Alice,' she answered. 'I expect—well, maybe. But can you imagine a stern sergeant of police turning up and arresting anyone at a CWA fête—and one put on to raise money to buy a special machine for the children's ward?' Clarissa was laughing openly now. Then she almost choked on catching sight of the apparition which had materialised from the corridor to the bedrooms.

'I don't believe it!' she exclaimed, and doubled up. Even Alice, so conservative and staid, was laughing. 'You really aren't going to go dressed in that get-up, are you, Sarah?' she asked.

'Of course I am! Don't you think I look marvellous—and so like a gypsy.' Sarah had on a long black wig that hid her own bright hair and great big gold loops dangling from her ear-lobes. She had also added a full multi-coloured skirt swirling about her ankles. All these, coupled with the heavy make-up she had used, certainly helped to give the impression of a real live gypsy.

But Alice was pointing. She gasped, her voice going high, 'You're definitely not going to wear that blouse, Sarah. You wouldn't dare—it's indecent!'

The would-be gypsy swung round in a swirling pirouette. And then, facing them both, she said laughingly, 'No, I don't think I would. I wouldn't mind doing it. But I expect I'd be sent home to change. I only put it on to see the kind of reception I got from you.'

'Well, you certainly got one,' grinned Clarissa, gazing at the blouse in question. It was made of the sheerest muslin and was quite see-through. And under it, Sarah wore nothing at all.

'Oh, well, the blouse was just to shock you. All the other is dressing up for my stall and to help Mrs Grady. Don't you think I really look the part?'

Both girls facing her nodded. Clarissa said, 'But you're not going to actually tell fortunes, are you? With Mrs

Grady, I expect it's all right. Even such a newcomer as I have heard of her—not that I believe in any such foolishness, because I don't. But you, Sarah . . .'

'Well . . .' Sarah swirled her colourful skirt about her and said, again gleefully, 'I might take some of the younger ones, reading their Tarot cards.'

'You can't, Sarah!' Alice's voice rose in a scandalised shout. 'Mrs Grady does have some kind of a reputation—even if we all take her prophecies with the proverbial grain of salt! But *you* can't do it.'

'OK, I know. But I'll tell you what, you two. I'll read your futures in the Tarot cards.'

'You'll do no such thing as far as I'm concerned,' replied Clarissa sharply, all amusement gone with the wind. She had no intention of allowing anyone, Mrs Grady included, to find the means to ferret around in her future.

The next day they found there weren't a thousand things to do; but there certainly were a hundred and one. But finally, at eleven o'clock, they were setting out their stall amid the bustle and laughter, the calling of enquiring voices, the endeavour to make their wares attractive.

But it was the colour all about them that gave the day its magic. The vivid emerald of the thick velvet lawn beneath them, the beds of tropical flowers and trees flaunting their blazing scarlets and pinks, the eye-catching stripes and designs of the big open umbrellas—and, most of all, it was the hurrying figures of the young nurses with their brilliant crimson shoulder capes over crisp white uniforms that added the final touch to what this fête was all about.

Clarissa was busy selling the small sailor suit when, glancing up, she saw the group of dignitaries pause beside their stall. She stood back, allowing Alice to reply to their greetings. She smiled when Dr Thornton spoke to her, looked blankly at his wife and Lesley Armitage, who weren't greeting her; smiled at the President of the CWA, and then they were gone.

Then, just before one o'clock, thanking the young nurse

who had just arrived with a tray of tea and sandwiches, they smiled at Sarah, as she also came to join them for their scratch meal.

'We've been invited to an impromptu dance, here at the quarters tonight,' began their gypsy when they were once more alone for a few minutes. Happily eating her sandwich, she continued, 'They've decided to put it on as a thank-you to all the helpers for such a successful day. That is, for anyone who wants to come. I know you're not going, Alice, because Eddie's working, but I've got a crowd together,' here Sarah smiled gleefully at the other two, before continuing, 'and we'll have a ball!'

'I don't know if you're including me in all this, Sarah.' It was with care that Clarissa chose her words, because she didn't know what she would be getting into.

'Oh, Clarissa, of course you have to come! I need you! I've met the dishiest kind of policeman . . .' Sarah's gleeful smile turned to laughter. 'He came looking into our tent. He spoke to me, glanced around, smiled, then walked out. I followed—and invited him to this affair tonight. After all, he is a helper. He gave his time free today, to walk around, showing the face of law and order. And then,' Sarah began ticking off her fingers, 'there's Stan, two girls from your school, Alice, Ted Ferguson and Jim Henson . . .'

'Why in the name of goodness is Jim included among you? I didn't see him working today. Anyway, I thought he played cricket at weekends,' interrupted Clarissa, to be interrupted in her turn.

'Yes, he does play cricket. But his mother is on the CWA committee, and he was roped in to work last night and this morning. So you have to come and make up the numbers, Clarissa.

'But I must say,' Sarah was continuing, 'that it's too bad that there are no young and charming doctors we can include . . . however, we'll certainly make do with what we've got.'

'Surely you're forgetting, Sarah,' Clarissa's tone held

saccharine sweetness, 'we do have a young and charming doctor.'

Sarah looked hard at her, frowning, sure that she wouldn't have missed such a one—and then the light dawned. 'Phooey!' she exclaimed. 'I don't count Lesley Armitage as young and charming!'

Clarissa laughed outright—at the tone, at the words. Lesley was young, and she was charming—to the people she considered it was worth the effort to be charming to.

'Look,' Sarah came suddenly upright, 'there's my relief waving to me, and you must admit that *she* doesn't look like a gypsy!'

The two girls left behind as she hurried away smiled at one another, both probably thinking the same thought. Life, for Sarah, was something to go through enjoying oneself, and if that didn't happen naturally, then it was one's duty to make it happen.

Around three o'clock they were on their way home. The small garments were all sold, the stall tidied up waiting to be moved. But, passing it, they saw a queue still waiting their turn at the fortune-teller's tent. Sarah wouldn't be going home just yet.

Sinking down on the sofa while Alice shut the door of the house behind them, Clarissa remarked speculatively, 'You know, I really don't know if I want to go tonight.'

'Oh, you'll enjoy yourself. I've been to affairs at the nurses' quarters. They have a great time, but of course there's always someone senior present because of its being held where it is. And you know Sarah—the crowd she gets around her always enjoy themselves.'

'Yes, I expect they do . . . and that I will too. OK!' Clarissa rose and wended her way to her bedroom.

It was about two hours later that her reading was interrupted. Sarah came in like a whirlwind. 'Look, Clarissa,' she said breathlessly, 'I'm going to have a long soap-bubble bath, then dress. I've been asked to help get things ready, and Phil is calling for me . . .'

'Who in the name of goodness is Phil?' asked Clarissa, gazing over the top of her book.

'Oh,' impatiently a hand was waved at her, 'Phil is the dishy policeman—I told you abut him. Well, he's coming too, to help Stan and the others prepare everything. So we're going early. But I've arranged for Jim Henson to call for you later. Right?'

'I suppose so.' Jim was someone Clarissa could feel comfortable with. But she did say to the girl now hurrying through the doorway, 'Mightn't Jim have other ideas about tonight for himself? I know your habit of rough-riding over everything and everyone to get your own way, Sarah.'

'Phooey!' Sarah retorted for the second time. 'He's delighted to come and get you.'

Clarissa lay back quietly, but now she wasn't reading. She was thinking, and of course it was of Alexis, wondering what he was doing at this moment. He should be home soon. The fortnight was almost up.

She drew in a breath of the fragrance wafting from beneath the bathroom door and into her room. Sarah was certainly laying it on! That aroma emanated from her most expensive oil. She saw Alice passing down the corridor, then heard a mumble of voices, then Alice was standing in her doorway. 'Will scrambled eggs be OK for tea, Clarissa?' she asked. 'Sarah doesn't want to eat, so I thought we'd just have an easy meal.'

'Of course—anything.'

'Right. I'll call you when it's ready.'

Deciding she would have to stop thinking of Alexis, because the thoughts went round and round until she was in his arms, feeling his body holding hers, feeling his lips trailing across bare skin until it was cool no longer, Clarissa abruptly swung her feet off the bed and walked down to Sarah's room.

'You smell nice,' she said.

Sarah turned, laughing. 'Oh, well,' she answered, 'you have to make time when it's there to be made.' She began to finish her make-up.

Glancing at the white dress hanging from the front of the wardrobe, suddenly Clarissa smiled, and, catching sight of it in the mirror, again Sarah turned. 'What are you planning, Clarissa? I know that look!'

Really astonished, Clarissa asked, 'What look? What are you on about?'

'The one you just had. As if you knew something no one else did. You don't have a lot to say, I realise that, but you get a look sometimes . . .'

'Don't be silly, Sarah!' Clarissa spoke curtly, even angrily, remembering suddenly that Alexis had told her about a look she had.

She said now, even more curtly, 'I was only looking at your dress. Are you planning to wear it?'

'Yes, I am.' Sarah turned to glance at it, but observing nothing wrong as it hung there in its pristine white freshness, she fixed the girl standing in her doorway with an old-fashioned look.

Clarissa put up a hand palm outwards in a peace gesture. She said, 'I was only thinking . . . I thought that maybe, as this is in some way a hospital affair, Lesley might be there, and . . .'

'Oh dear—I didn't think of that! That would spoil the whole night!'

'She probably wouldn't wear her white dress, and she might even not be there . . .'

'It doesn't matter,' Sarah interrupted. 'I'm not risking it.' Rummaging through her wardrobe, she brought out a green and white linen. 'Actually,' she remarked, 'I think I like this one on me even better.' And, happy again, she slipped it over her head.

'There's tea ready. I'd better go and eat it or I'll be in trouble,' said Clarissa as Alice called again impatiently.

Absently eating the scrambled eggs, unaware of even tasting the appetising concoction, suddenly Clarissa put down her fork. She didn't think she had any special look.

She was reserved, she knew, and had been told so forcefully on occasions by other students she had dated. But of course that hadn't mattered. Through all these years only one man had mattered. And only one man mattered now.

Her name being spoken across from her didn't even register; it did, however, the second time it came. Glancing up through downcast lashes, abruptly she remembered, and looked up properly. 'Sorry,' she smiled over at Alice, 'I must have been miles away. What was it you said?'

Alice shifted a little in her chair as if she were uncomfortable, then said more than a trifle hesitantly, 'Look, Clarissa—we three get on very well, don't we?'

Astonished for the second time tonight, Clarissa nodded, saying, 'Yes, of course. Why?'

'Well, I don't want to pry, but I've noticed sometimes that though your body may be here, your mind and thoughts simply are not. Is something troubling you, or did you leave someone down in Brisbane who you're unhappy about? You're so attractive, yet you seem interested in no one, and take up none of the passes made at you.'

'For heaven's sake, Alice, you're making me blush! And thank you. I do know it's only concern for me that makes you ask. But no, I didn't leave anyone behind in Brisbane, and—this is only for you—I am in love with someone, but I don't know if anything will ever come of it.'

'But why ever not? You're quite lovely, Clarissa! And nice with it. I can't imagine any man not wanting you! Unless——' Alice's words halted abruptly, then with a shrug, she continued, 'unless, of course, he's already married, or in love with someone else.'

And, blindingly, an idea flowered in Clarissa's mind. *Was* Alexis in love with someone else, even maybe still with Delys, or with someone a difficulty existed about? That would explain his attitude—an explanation she had simply never thought of. There *did* exist a kind of electricity between them, enough feeling for Alexis to make love to her completely. Both of them knew that. However, he thought

of her, and had told her so, as being young. And, coupled
with that other incident which had happened so long ago,
being Alexis, always scrupulous, he wouldn't have an affair
with her that would only be that—an affair!

Suddenly, with frightening brightness, she knew that this
was probably so, that between her and Alexis there would
never now be anything; and an abyss of desolation welled up
within her. She had had hope before, of there being some
kind of togetherness, because she had known as the years
passed that without him she would always be alone, that
there would be no one else.

But she had never thought of this. She had naturally
thought that if Alexis wanted anybody, being who he was,
what he was, they would be his merely for the asking.

Her head went down on a supporting elbow. She wasn't
even aware of where she was. Alexis' face was before her, so
close, and of all the many expressions she had seen on it, this
time she imagined it held one of repudiation, even if it also
held one of regret.

'Clarissa . . . Clarissa!' The urgency in Alice's tone
recalled her to the present.

'Sorry,' she told the anxious face opposite. 'I was just
thinking. But there's no need for you to look like that. And
no, he's not married. But you could be right with your
second sentence, he may well be in love with someone else.
Now let's talk about something more interesting.'
Determinedly she picked up her fork.

Their light meal finished, they were tidying the kitchen
when they heard the car pull up. Alice called Sarah's name,
then went to open the door.

He was nice, Sarah's dishy policeman. Tanned face
smiling, he greeted them before turning as Sarah walked
into the lounge, bringing with her the enveloping fragrance
of perfume.

Their visitor took hold of her hand, grinning openly at
her. 'I expect,' he said, 'that you're my date. But you don't
look at all like the gypsy I made the engagement with.'

They all laughed, and Sarah flipped a hand to Alice, saying over a departing shoulder to Clarissa, 'See you later!'

Glancing at her watch, Alice moved in the direction of the bedrooms, saying, 'It's after six-thirty, Clarissa. I expect you're going to get ready. I'm going to try to turn that material of mine into a Christian Dior creation.'

'And do you know what, Alice? I think you're going to do it. You've cut it out and the material is fabulous.' Clarissa turned into her own bedroom.

As Sarah had, she rummaged through her wardrobe, and at the back of it she stroked the sunshine yellow dress. Well, that was one garment she wasn't going to wear tonight. Or the creation which her mother had bought as a going-away present for her—and definitely was only to be worn for a very special occasion.

She gazed at it, wondering now if after that conversation at the tea-table she would ever wear it up here. Fashioned in what looked like a soft silk linen and sliced sideways over the bustline, it exposed one shoulder, and had a two-inch border of vividly coloured embroidery across the gleaming white bodice. A skirt that was only slightly flared to allow freedom of movement also had a band of the same intensely coloured work at the hemline. With a twisted cord of threaded gold to turn about the waist, it could have been worn in ancient Greece.

Clarissa ran it back on the rail and took out a flowered cotton. Tonight was just an impromptu affair, and though it was a casual frock, she liked this one. Midnight blue with large white flowers scattered widely over it, it had a low, scooped neckline and a wide flared skirt. She hung it on the outside of the wardrobe, then, collecting her toiletries, made for the bathroom.

Turning on the shower-taps, she smiled. There was to be no bubble-bath tonight for her. A hot shower, followed by a cold one, with Cussons' soap for fragrance, was all she was allowing herself. And it was just on seven-thirty when she picked up her small evening purse and flicked out her bedroom light. Calling goodnight to Alice, and receiving only a mumbled reply, she walked through into the lounge.

Oh good, she thought, hearing a car drive up. Both of us on time. She walked through to the front veranda, slamming the door shut behind her. Smiling, she walked out to meet the figure running up the steps.

CHAPTER NINE

ABRUPTLY, unexpectedly, her feet dragged to a complete halt. Her wide, friendly smile slipping, she made herself try to keep some of it on her face.

'Good evening, Clarissa,' said Federico Martinez. 'Behold your transport!'

Still keeping her smile from sliding away, Clarissa asked, 'Where's Jim Henson?'

'Oh,' an arm propelled widely in a throw away gesture, a smile was directed at her, and he said, 'I really don't go into all these things, Clarissa. However, I think I heard somewhere that he had transport problems too. So I was roped in. Ready?'

But still she stood, then found herself saying, 'I would have thought you would never allow yourself to be in a position that could even remotely suggest that you were available for anyone's transport.'

'As you say, I don't put myself in such a position—but then I'm not in that sort of position now. When I found out, in all the hullabaloo going on, who it was that needed to be collected, I was very pleased to offer my services. Now, are you ready?' Federico asked again, and half turned, waiting for her to precede him down the steps.

Clarissa still couldn't make her legs move towards him. But what was she to do? To say she had changed her mind about going when she was already dressed and ready was simply out of the question. That would be an insult to any man!

Federico turned, looking at her, and across the yards separating them she saw those tawny lion's eyes. She also saw in them the knowledge that he was well aware of her unwillingness. He smiled, and said for the third time, 'Ready?'

What else could she do but what she did, so she smiled at him and said, 'Yes, thank you,' and walked before him down the steps.

Seating her in the passenger side of the low sports car, Federico went round and slid behind the wheel. Leaning across, he said, 'Let me,' and, taking hold of her seat-belt, clipped it shut. Carelessly she watched as he attended to his own, and wondered how in the name of heaven this situation had arisen, out of the blue when she could really do nothing about it.

She looked at the heavy body which seemed so close in the small confines of the front seat, and she knew why Alexis had warned her. Federico *was* attractive, and he *was* used to getting his own way, but he also carried around him an element of unsheathed menace. She wished they would hurry up and get to the nurses' quarters. That was the one thought in her mind.

She hadn't noticed a long grey car easing into the kerb as it came level with their house, and then stop completely on observing the vehicle already parked there, the driver of it watching her being ushered inside by its owner.

She also didn't see that as it began to follow them, a large truck swung round Federico's small foreign car, and coasted into the next-door driveway, blocking the path of the Jaguar, cutting it off.

She did say carefully to her own driver, 'Have you missed the turning, Federico? We went on that road back there when Alice drove us today.'

'I've just got something to pick up. It won't take a moment.' A friendly smile was sent her way, and then suddenly they were through the town and out on the main highway. She mustn't panic, Clarissa was telling herself. She said quietly, 'This isn't the way. Where are we going?'

The man turned and, again smiling at her, put out a hand to place it over one of her own. 'No worries. We're just going home for a pre-dance drink. We won't take long—and it's one way of getting to know you.'

She could go. She could also ignore the stares she would receive, turning up with Fred Martinez an hour or two after he had left to collect her. So she watched the road, the glaring headlights coming towards them. Then, as the little car slowed down to take a wide curve, she snapped open the catch of her seatbelt, pressed the door-handle—with an inward prayer that it wasn't locked from the dashboard like the Jaguar's doors could be—and threw herself out.

They had been slowing for a corner, and the car was low-slung, but a cry was forced from her as her shoulder hit the road, with her left leg dragging hard over the bitumen. Then she had fallen off the built-up edge and into the ditch beyond.

Getting up clumsily, she couldn't prevent the cry that escaped her, and every jolting step she made herself take sent a stabbing fire through her shoulder. Reaching the cane, she moved as far and as fast as she could along its outer edge, then the sound of a car door slamming sent her scurrying into its close-growing clumps for concealment.

She heard the heavy, hurrying footsteps negotiate the ditch, then come onward . . . up and down from where she had fallen. Then his voice called to her, 'What a bloody stupid thing to do, Clarissa! It *was* meant to be only a drink before going on. Come on out now and I'll take you home.'

Holding her rasping breath, holding also the arm lying across her chest in an endeavour to protect the wounded shoulder, Clarissa kept as still as she could. That voice calling to her had carried a note of violent anger, and she had no intention of getting again into that car idling now on the road beyond them.

He came again to the edge of the field where she was standing, walking up and down it, even edging inside, and she thanked goodness she had worn the dark-coloured

dress that she had. She was frightened now. Fred had a
right to be angry—and he was! He wasn't to know the
reason she couldn't allow herself to go to his house—for
only a drink, or anything else. That it was the
remembrance of a low, uncompromising voice, warning
her.

He was muttering as he searched; a growling mutter,
but she couldn't understand it. It could have been any of
three languages—Greek, Spanish, or even English. Then
she did hear words, and they were in English—something
about a light, and he had turned, hurrying away.

Unaware if he was departing or not, Clarissa scrambled
out of the cane, biting her lip as each step jolted her
shoulder, and moved as swiftly as she could along its
edge. But again hearing a car door slam, and seeing the
bobbing of an electric torch as Federico jumped the ditch
to begin his searching once more, she moved into the
heavy green foliage again.

Sick with the thought of the scene which would ensue if
she was discovered, she acknowledged that what she had
done had been foolish, and she could understand him
being furious. He certainly sounded it, as he searched
along and even into the cane, then called out again,
'Don't be a fool, Clarissa! This is bloody stupid! Come on
out and I'll take you home.'

But she had looked into those eyes of his on two
occasions, so she stayed motionless, frightened now.
There came a scraping noise sounding close which almost
caused her to cry out. There were snakes in these close-
growing fields . . . and rats.

Then after what seemed hours, but most likely was only
minutes, he was going away, and the words echoing back
to her she probably wouldn't want to understand anyway.
They were swear-words, she knew, in whatever language
they were being uttered.

She heard the car start, but swinging round, it was
being driven slowly along until the fields ended and the

streets of the town began.

Also leaving, Clarissa walked as fast as pain allowed her to. She could go home by the back streets, which would be no distance at all, she told herself hardily.

It wasn't far either, and carefully, her arm held tightly, she arrived finally at the house backing on to their own. Going down the side, she came to the hibiscus hedge, and pushed until she could squeeze sideways through the opening in it.

Going even more carefully now after this endeavour, each step accompanied by a darting stab of fire, Clarissa walked up the back steps, hoping that the kitchen door had not been locked yet—then wondered fleetingly where her evening purse was resting at this moment.

As it happened, the knob yielded easily to her hand, and inside, she switched on the light. She gazed down at the trickle of moisture which she knew had been easing down her leg, and saw that it was blood. Reaching for a paper towel, she patted at it to stop its journey on to the clean floor. She glanced up and saw Alice in the doorway.

'In the name of goodness, what have you been doing to yourself!' The exclamation came, horrified.

Rising from trying to mop up the blood which seemed to be escaping as if from a hand-grenade wound, Clarissa saw the expression on her friend's face—and started to giggle, exhaustion, pain, and fright bringing on incipient hysteria.

Sharply she made herself stop. 'Look, Alice,' she told the girl in the doorway, 'I've been in an accident. Do you think you could ring that doctor you made me register with when I first came up here? I've either dislocated my collarbone or broken it.'

For a short moment Alice remained silent, then in an altogether different tone she spoke. 'Yes, of course. But you'll have to tell me what happened. Were you . . . who have you been with? One look at you now and the doctor might well call the police—and *I* don't want a scandal!'

For a second time that low, uncontrollable laughter surfaced, and to stop it Clarissa drew a deep ragged breath. 'Look,' she said, 'it's really not as bad as it seems. And I haven't been hurt in the way you might be thinking of, or in the way I look could suggest.'

Clarissa gazed down at herself. Her low neckline had burst asunder and was hanging on threads, exposing her shoulder and the white bra; the skirt on the left side was frayed and rent as if with heavy scorch-marks. Then with the ghost of a shrug that sent pain through her hurt shoulder, she continued,

'Did you say *you* don't want any scandal? Well, I'm telling you that I don't either. I'll tell you what happened if you promise, on your honour, not to breathe one word of it. Not even to Eddie, to whom of course you would normally tell everything.'

Suddenly her lids fell over exhausted eyes. The enormity of such a tale going the rounds of the hospital appalled her. Everyone would be laughing, and the kids at school. And Federico . . . heavens, he would murder her! She would have to fake some sort of a story.

'Just tell me and I'll see!' Alice's tone was uncompromising.

They stood gazing at one another, both thinking of their own futures. Clarissa said helplessly, 'I couldn't bear it all to come out.'

'All right. Look, Eddie is in for that big promotion, and *I* don't want anything I'm involved with to go even near him,' replied Alice, her voice hard. 'So just tell me.'

'Oh, of course.' Relief surged through Clarissa. 'Well then, Jim Henson didn't call for me tonight. Federico Martinez did.'

'Federico Martinez? How on earth does he come within our orbit?'

'I think . . . I think maybe he was a little attracted to me . . . Oh, for heaven's sake, Alice!' continued Clarissa on seeing the expression that crept across the other girl's face. 'It was probably just that he saw me as someone different. It was at Alexis' barbecue, and the look with which he acknowledged the introduction wasn't just a polite one, you know . . .'

Alice did know, but she only said, 'Yes, go on.'

'Well, I'd been warned against him, and when he offered me a lift home from church one Sunday, I refused. Oh, I refused charmingly—really, no one could have taken umbrage. And then . . . and then . . .' Clarissa found she needed to take a deep breath to carry on, 'when I went outside tonight, I found it was Federico who'd come calling for me—not Jim Henson.

'What could I do? I really didn't want to go with him. Do you know, apart from being warned about him, I really am a little scared of him. But I couldn't refuse to go, of course I couldn't, and knowing that, he was laughing at me.'

'Did he attack you? No, I can't believe that. I do know his reputation. But he lives in this town, Clarissa, and from what I've heard—and we've all heard about him in such a small community as this—he doesn't need to resort to rape to further his love affairs. He *is* a very attractive man, you know—as well as being a very wealthy and experienced one.'

'I know all that. And I sense the attraction, but I would always tread warily around him. And of course he didn't attack me. He was quite charming, but he wouldn't take me straight to the hospital dance. He just said he was taking me to his place for a pre-dance drink. And that probably was all he intended. But, Alice, can you imagine me walking into that affair with him a couple of hours after he'd left to call for me? I can.' A convulsive shudder ran through Clarissa at the thought of Lesley Armitage and Mrs Thornton looking them both over, and even of Sarah's mischievous laughing look.

'Oh yes, I can imagine. But what did you do? How did you get in this mess?'

'I unzipped my seat-belt, pressed down the door handle and threw myself out.'

'Oh, heavens! You might have been killed!'

If Clarissa had been appalled previously when thinking of Federico's reaction to such a tale going the rounds, Alice was now simply aghast.

But Clarissa replied carelessly, 'I didn't think I would be; we were slowing for a curve, and that car of his is practically on the ground, you know. Anyway, I didn't think of the consequences . . . and I didn't care about them either.'

'But . . . but . . .' Alice was beyond speech.

'So I picked myself out of the ditch where I'd landed and hobbled for the cane-fields as fast as I could.'

'But Federico . . . surely he didn't just leave you?'

'No, of course he didn't.' Clarissa shivered, remembering the sound of his voice while he had been searching. 'He came looking for me, and he was *furious*! He sounded so angry—in all sorts of languages . . .'

'I just bet he did!'

'Well, in the end he drove away, looking for me in the streets, I guess. I came the back way. Now, are you going to keep quiet about the whole rotten affair?'

'Of course I am—it would be a scandal. Look, we have to get a doctor for you, and we have to make up a story for all of us.' And, bending their imagination to it, that was just what they did.

Wasn't she thankful for Alice! A little giggle escaped Clarissa, and this time it wasn't one of incipient hysteria. It was at the iron-hard determination which her friend was displaying; doing what Clarissa had once accused Sarah of doing—riding roughshod over everything which might come, even remotely, near the big promotion Eddie was in for.

She had gone and phoned the doctor, returning with her dressmaking scissors. A raised eyebrow was sent Clarissa's way, but she only nodded. Then the blades sheared through a dress she wouldn't have been able to take off even if it had been worth saving—which it was not.

Again that silly giggle erupted, and she said, 'If I go on having to discard dresses every time I go out, I'll soon need a new wardrobe!'

'In that case, let's hope you don't get another through the post; because the less that's known about this dreadful accident the better I'll be pleased. And I'm also informing you, Clarissa,' added Alice abrasively, 'that that includes Sarah as well. Good heavens, just imagine the time she'd have with such a story!'

Appalled yet once again tonight, Clarissa answered forcefully, 'Too right, I can just imagine!'

Cleaned up, she had a story prepared for the doctor, which, if he didn't altogether believe it, he didn't dispute, because Clarissa's wounded shoulder could have been caused by falling down the high front steps. Her leg could have also been grazed by splintered wood and hard concrete.

An injection took care of the pain when her shoulder was put back where it was supposed to be and then her arm put in a sling. The doctor only remarked, while cleaning and bandaging it, that she would need to be careful about the leg, but if she did as she was told, they would have it well in no time.

He had snapped shut his bag, handed Clarissa two pills to take before sleeping, said he would see her at the surgery on Monday, added a goodnight, and left.

He didn't hear the two heartfelt sighs of relief that followed his departing figure, or see the man who stepped out from a low-slung car parked some distance away and ran up the stairs he had just descended.

'Well, that's that!' It was with satisfaction that Alice spoke the few words, and she was turning away when a sharp knock came upon the door. The two girls looked a trifle apprehensively at one another, then, as a second knock echoed through the air-waves about them—a much more peremptory one this time, Alice walked across to open the door.

Because she had no choice, she moved back abruptly, pushed aside by the man who strode in. He glanced around the room and saw Clarissa by the kitchen doorway, holding the thin housecoat around her half-clothed figure.

Those tawny eyes looked her over, and suddenly it wasn't like down among the cane when she could only hear his angry voice. This time she suffered the full glance of a furious, enraged look.

'So you got home, did you? While I've been out searching the streets. I could actually murder you, let me tell you! What a stupid thing to do! You could have been killed, and then where would I have been?'

Abruptly, in a room which had anger and menace colouring its whole atmosphere, Clarissa began to laugh.

Alice said, 'Stop it, Clarissa!'

'Yes . . . yes, all right! It's just that . . . Did you wonder what was going to be the papers' headlines tomorrow, Federico?'

'Yes, I did wonder! And it wasn't in case of any gossip going the rounds, my reputation would stand any of that, but if you'd been badly hurt, that's a different matter altogether. Good lord . . . a girl thrown out of my car!' His next words weren't in English, and this time Clarissa recognised that they were in Greek.

'Well, Federico,' she made herself speak against the furious anger which still seemed to envelop his taut figure and said, 'I imagine our reputations wouldn't stand the kind of reception such a story would engender. We're schoolteachers, you know, so we decided that I'd slipped and fallen down the high front steps.'

An arrested expression came to take away some of the glaring anger in those tawny eyes, and his glance roved over her, over the arm in a sling, the bandages covering from knee to calf. He said sarcastically, 'And how did the doctor take that?'

Relief flooded through Clarissa at his reaction. She said carefully, 'A dislocated collarbone could easily ensue from falling down a steep flight of stairs . . . and my leg got grazed on the wooden steps and hard cement beneath them. So now, please, will you do something for me?'

The smile he bestowed on her was the one he used to charm. He replied, 'Can I say yes . . . anything!'

'Then I'd like you to go back to that dance; and if anyone asks about me, or about you coming here . . .'

'My dear Clarissa, need I remind you that no one asks me questions if I don't want to be asked them.'

'Coming to know you a little more, especially after tonight, Federico, no, I don't expect you do. However,' astringency was the tone her voice carried now, 'I don't want you to act like that. So could you just say impatiently something about an accident, or a doctor, and shrug. Now, that should be in character, shouldn't you think?'

'Oh, yes, I expect I could manage that. An expression of impatience is one of my favourite ploys.'

It was over! Abruptly the room around Clarissa began to weave up and down in the most amazing fashion. She slumped against the wall at her back, thinking that possibly this could be the result of that injection the doctor had given her while fixing her arm. She heard Alice say, 'Look, Federico, Clarissa's all in. I'll get her to bed. Goodnight.'

'All right. I'll come and see how things are tomorrow.'

'Oh, no, you won't! That would be definitely out of character. You just keep well away from here, do you understand?'

He understood her, and left. Clarissa didn't hear him go. On rubbery legs she went away on Alice's arm, took

her pills and dropped from this traumatic night into deep,
faraway oblivion.

CHAPTER TEN

THE GIRL in the sunlight-flooded room moved restlessly, then came awake as the outside sounds penetrated her drug-induced sleep. And suddenly she was wide awake, memory of the happenings of last night surfacing. She stretched now, and called out, and it was Sarah who opened the door. 'Hi, there,' she greeted. 'What's the idea of having an accident and missing such a beaut dance?'

'But you didn't miss a beaut partner, did you, Sarah?' asked Clarissa, well aware that this question would send her friend's thoughts to her own concerns. It did!

'No, I didn't. And I'm going down to the beach with him today.'

'Be that as it may, but for now you're coming in to breakfast. I don't want it getting cold.' It was Alice speaking, gazing at Clarissa over the clustering red curls of the other girl.

Clarissa nodded, and with a long nightdress hiding all her bandages, she swung herself out of bed.

She spent the rest of the day there, and it wasn't her shoulder that kept her in bed, but the aching of her leg. She went to the surgery on Monday, had it dressed, and was told to go home and come back on Thursday.

And on Thursday her arm came out of the sling, and the thick bandages on her leg were reduced to pads and plaster strapping. On Friday she went to work. And that, she thought, was the end of that horrendous week.

It was on that afternoon, after getting her lessons checked and returned to her, that Clarissa walked through the waning afternoon a little later than normal. Secure in the knowledge that the heavy denim skirt swinging about

her ankles—which she had routed out from among her
city clothes—was doing what was expected of it, hiding
any signs of bandaging, she walked slowly home.

Also, the denim skirt didn't come amiss. Tomorrow
was the first of June; the beginning of what passed for
winter this far north. And although it was not cold, it was
pleasant walking now, and there might soon be the need
for a jumper at night.

Her face upturned to the evening breeze which had just
sprung up, Clarissa sauntered slowly along, still careful of
her shoulder and leg . . . and thought of Alexis,
wondering what he was doing at this moment. He had
said in his letter, about ten days or a fortnight, but that
time had passed and it was now into three weeks. Still,
that fact had been a fortunate bonus, she had thought a
dozen times these last few days, giving fervent thanks that
he had been away during that traumatic time.

Her lids fell as that so vividly remembered image swam
before her vision. And, thinking of him, she was unaware
of a car which was easing into the kerb beside her.
Vehicles were always passing up and down on this road in
either direction.

However, she did glance down when it stopped beside
her, and it was as if a dream had taken on reality. The
driver of it was leaning across to swing wide the passenger
side door.

Happily she went into the long grey car, and not even
waiting to shut the door, turned sideways to exclaim,
'Alexis! Have you just got back?'

'No, I haven't just got back. Shut the door, please!'

'Oh, of course.' Clarissa turned, pulling it closed, and,
gathering up her seat-belt, she clipped it firmly. Then
turning to him with a radiant smile on her face, she asked,
'When did you get back, Alexis?'

'A week or so ago.'

Abruptly, unexpectedly, Clarissa noted the atmosphere
about them, and looked more searchingly at her

companion—and found she was gazing at a face altogether different from the one she carried in her memory bank. What on earth could be wrong?

She asked carefully, 'Did your business go all right, Alexis?'

'As well as could be expected!' answered this stranger beside her.

Clarissa didn't realise that her lids had come down to guard her eyes, and that she was glancing over at him from under downcast lashes.

Apparently the driver of the big car did. He uttered a short sound which could—with some imagination—be taken as a laugh. He said, 'Didn't I tell you once before that that little gesture of yours is very well practised?'

Not knowing whether to be angry, because it wasn't a practised gesture, or astonished that he could speak to her in that tone, Clarissa drew back into her own corner.

What could be the matter? Why was Alexis behaving like this? It was so unlike a man who was almost always charming—to everyone.

Her eyes opened properly now, she glanced at him, and a tinge of apprehension went through her. That face beside her appeared carved in stone, rigid and rock-hard, coloured in ebony one moment, then bronzed golden the next, as the Jaguar fled between horizontal sun-rays slanting low and the long darkening shadows that built-up areas flung wide.

It seemed again the face of a menacing stranger.

Then, shatteringly, a reason for this behaviour came to her. She asked carefully, 'Has something happened about your business affairs, Alexis, or is there trouble with your cane?'

'Oh no, my business affairs, as you call them, are perfectly well . . . and I've never had a better crop of cane.'

'Well then, what's the matter?'

'Should something be the matter, my dear Clarissa?'

Something certainly was the matter, speaking to her as he did in that fashion.

Beginning to get a little angry herself, she replied, 'Your attitude makes it seem so. But no worries. Here's my street coming up. Thank you for the lift.'

The turn into her street *was* coming up, and she went to unclip her seat-belt, wanting to be out of this car as soon as it stopped . . . wanting to be away from this so different Alexis. Suddenly, tears stung behind her eyelids, but she blinked them fiercely back. She wasn't going to cry over any man, she decided angrily. And certainly not over this one, after she had gone through all the worry and pain of this last week—for which, she thought astringently, he was partly to blame.

Then suddenly she wondered if he had met some other woman he had become attracted to. And, being Alexis, as there *had* been some kind of rapport between them, he had come along to tell her in the privacy of this drive.

Oh, well, she thought, that was nothing new in her young life. Most likely it would be harder to get over this time, having been held in his arms, having been kissed . . . Her body came upright with a jerk, sending memories flying.

From thinking of that, and at this particular time, she said, keeping a shake out of her voice, 'There's my street now, Alexis.'

It was, but they were past it. She said again, 'You missed my street, Alexis,' and on receiving no reply a sense of déjà vu began to overtake her. They were the words she had used to Federico on that dreadful Saturday night.

But this was Alexis, not Federico. She added, 'You can turn in the next street and go back that way.'

'I haven't missed the street. We're going out to my home for a while.'

Clarissa almost replied, her control slipping, 'Surely not for a pre-dance drink?' and made herself push back the small half-hysterical laugh that was trying to escape her.

What would he say if he knew about that escapade? This time it was not merely a tinge of apprehension that went through her entire metabolism, but a small shiver of fear. But he couldn't know. No one did.

She heard herself saying, 'But why your place, Alexis? You could take me to my home if there's anything you wanted to discuss with me.' *Was* it some other woman?

'Oh, yes, I do have something to discuss with you. But I would rather do it where we won't be interrupted . . .' Alexis broke off, watching the cars as he cut across the main highway traffic and into his own private roadway.

Clarissa also fell silent. It would come soon enough, what it was he wanted to say to her.

Alexis reached up to pull down the sun-visor. They were driving straight into the brightness of the blazing orb lying low now just above the horizon. Even as she watched, Clarissa saw it slip even lower into what was going to be a vivid sunset.

Then they were at the farm, driving around to the back entrance, and Alexis was pulling up beside the barbecue area. Slipping out from behind the wheel, he came round to open her door.

Not wanting to alight, to go anywhere with this so different man, she said, 'Say what you have to, Alexis, then I can go home.'

Without replying, he leaned into the car, right across her, bending to unclip her seat-belt, and, gazing down at that brown head with its golden streaks, at the broad shoulders lying so close against her breast, she almost put out a hand to touch him.

There was no time. Belt unclipped, he stood back. But as she still made no effort to emerge from the car, he reached out a hand to grip and bring her to him.

Clarissa winced as those hard fingers pressed into her hurt shoulder, and stepped out as quickly as she could, in an endeavour to ease that pressure.

Alexis must have noticed. For the briefest second he stood, looking her over, then he said, 'My touch didn't at one time make you cringe—far from it. Is it that you've found someone else's touch more to your liking?'

'Don't be silly, Alexis.' And it was her tone which was carrying bleakness now. 'I just simply don't understand you this evening.'

'Come along then, and we'll try to arrive at an understanding. There are ways and means to decide everything.'

So, having no option, she went along beside him, along this area she remembered so vividly, to go through a door into a kitchen she also remembered, wishing he would take those hard, strong fingers away from her arm and shoulder. She had thought the thing was better, but that grip was hurting her. Well, it would have to hurt. She wasn't going to ask him to take it away—and explain why. Oh, no!

He reached down and closed the door as they went through it, then turning to her, he said, still in a voice, a tone, she didn't recognise, 'Come along to where it's more comfortable.'

His fingers had now let go her arm and shoulder, and with a gesture he indicated that she walk before him. However, they came to take hold of her once more as she made to move along the way she had traversed before when coming here wet through. And, unable to help it, she winced again as he swung her round by the shoulder in the opposite direction.

The room when they came to it was a large, a very large bedroom, and had an entire side of glass windows rising from top to bottom. It was as if one were living in open bushland amid the close-growing foliage of green. And through it all, scattered in profusion, was the vivid brightness that was the tropical flowers among it.

Clarissa said uncertainly, just for something to say,

'This room must have been modernised since the house was built. Mr Smith told me once it was nearly a hundred years old. In those days people didn't like living out of doors as much as the modern generation is inclined to do.'

Good heavens, she was babbling! She stopped, turning to look at him.

'I've noticed,' he told her, 'that you cringe away from my touch. Was Martinez' touch more to your liking?'

Shocked, absolutely aghast, she couldn't answer, couldn't make herself even breathe. It was as if someone had kicked her hard in the solar plexus, scattering her whole metabolism into fragments. Then the words did come out. 'What do you mean, Alexis? And why are you speaking to me in this manner?'

'I'm speaking to you in this fashion because I've come to realise how lacking in ordinary common sense I've been, how stupid I was to handle you so carefully. Because in spite of my warning, you chose Fred Martinez to go partying with. Did you enjoy yourself, Clarissa? Especially as it wasn't to a party that he took you. Oh, of course he carries an aura of magnetism about him, and of course he's very wealthy. Still, for girls like you he should be someone to be avoided! Because when *he* marries, as he will do, it will be to a woman chosen for that purpose—to someone belonging to his own circle.'

'I don't care who Federico Martinez marries. I can't understand you, Alexis. Look, I want to go home.'

He must have heard something about last Saturday night, she was thinking. But no, he couldn't have, she told herself definitely. No one had. Nothing had got out. And if Federico had told him about it, Alexis wouldn't be acting towards her the way he was, so she said again, 'I'd like to go home.'

'And so you shall. But first I'm going to do what I've wanted to do for four months . . . but because of an incident that happened long years ago, I decided that with someone as young and as inexperienced as you were then, this time I'd take things slowly.

'Inexperienced—oh, no!' He had reached out to bring her to him, completely into him, and with head descending, his lips came searching.

This was Alexis, she knew, to whom she would gladly give everything he wanted. But not like this. Oh, no, not like this! She said, turning her head sharply, 'Stop it, Alexis! And please tell me why you're acting like this?'

He straightened up. He stood motionless for the heartbeat of a second, though still keeping her clasped tightly within his hold. He said then, 'Very well. I'll tell you. No! I'll ask you one question. Did you go out with Fred last Saturday night? And did you not go to that dance at which you were expected?'

Her own eyes startled, wide open, Clarissa looked into slate-black eyes which had concentrated into brilliant diamond pinpoints. She said, 'Yes, I did, but it wasn't what you think. I . . .' She was trying to find words to explain. But Alexis didn't want to hear. His mouth came down to rest upon hers, to move slowly and expertly back and forth, over and across . . . Then, abruptly, those kisses that seemed to be finding their way, searching in remembrance, had changed, turning into deep, scorching caresses.

She jerked, getting her head free to turn her face, and heard again that strange laughter he had uttered in the Jaguar, a sound coming from deep within his throat. He said in not his own voice at all, 'This will do just as well,' and sent his lips plundering along the exposed thrown-back neckline, down, down to where the v of her blouse was buttoned.

Then she was swung up and dumped on the bed, and Alexis was gazing down at her. Frightened by that look, thinking that this scene was going much too far, she began trying to explain.

The backs of his fingers stroked down her cheek, as

they had done on another, very different occasion from this, stopped to press over her lips for the briefest second, then continued until they came to the buttons, and he began one by one to undo them all.

Endeavouring to sit upright, Clarissa said as sharply as she could make her voice speak, 'Stop it, Alexis! Whatever you think, right or not, gives you no excuse to behave as you are doing. Please take me home!'

'Certainly I'll take you home—but not now. Afterwards . . . oh, yes. Surely you don't think I'd want you to stay then? But for now . . .' His arm went beneath her to cradle her to him as his long hard body came to rest alongside, the hurt shoulder held imprisoned against his chest. He was kissing her now, with the kind of kisses she had never known existed, and which sent silver coils that unwound and jumped deep within her body.

Unable to move in that tight embrace, unable to resist those devastating caresses, she collapsed against him.

What caused him to stop, what caused his head to come up sharply, she didn't know. But she squeezed her eyes fiercely shut, not wanting him to see the tears she knew were there.

But he said, 'Surely not tears, Clarissa? Do you dislike my kisses so much? Well, we'll have to remedy that, won't we? And I'm sure I know the way to set about it.' His head was descending again.

Clarissa said, 'I'm not crying—I'm not! You wouldn't cause me to shed tears for you, Alexis Markham. I might have . . . have had some kind of feeling for you at one time, but after your behaviour of tonight, not any more, believe me!

'For you to even think what you *are* thinking about me shows how wrong I've been. Thank goodness that tonight has set me free of you. Now you can do what you like, but when it's over, I'll never willingly look in your direction again.'

'Oh, well, in that case, and as it won't mean so much to

you, I can begin to enjoy myself . . . indulge myself.'
Alexis went to lean across her, and the mattress moved as
his hand came down heavily on her shoulder. She cried
out, she couldn't prevent the sound erupting.

Abruptly, Alexis went immobile, and in the rapidly
darkening room, he gazed down at her as she lay
outspread beneath him. He reached up and switched on
the bedlight above. It came on blindingly, bathing them
both in its brilliance.

He looked at her, at the blouse, opened and pulled from
its waistband, at the rucked-up skirt, showing what it did.

For a full moment he remained still, then one finger
reached out to move a white bra strap. He said, 'What on
earth have you been doing to yourself? Your entire
shoulder isn't black and blue, but it's deep orange and
yellow!'

It was, she knew that. Because apart from her
dislocated collarbone, her shoulder muscles had also
crunched heavily on the road. She remained silent. And
as Alexis did too, she tried to bring the two sides of her
blouse together. But hard fingers prevented her from
doing so. 'Tell me first,' said a voice in a tone more like
the one he normally used.

What was she to say? She could tell him the tale
everyone knew. But he had told her once, in this very
house, that she would be unable to lie to him. She said
baldly, 'I had an accident.'

'So I supposed!' He had turned from her uncovered
body now to where the bandages showed beneath the
dishevelled skirt. He leant down over her to look at them
searchingly, touch one carefully, then said, 'Now, tell
me.'

He lifted her up and piled pillows behind her. 'Don't
think,' he told her, 'that I don't want to be told all about
Fred Martinez—because I do. I need to know. But first,
how did this happen to you, and why didn't you mention
it when I first hurt your shoulder?'

'I just had an accident. It's nothing. It's almost better. I really would like to go home.' And she did want to. All she wanted was to get away from someone she found now that she didn't even like. She added, hoping it would expedite matters, 'I feel sick. You hurt my shoulder!'

If she had expected sympathy, or to be let go, she was disappointed. Alexis said only, 'Don't change the subject. If you'd told me you had a sore shoulder, I wouldn't have hurt you. Now, explain to me about this accident.' He reached up and turned the angled lamp a fraction, and looked again at her shoulder.

'This happened days ago,' he said, 'so stop being so secretive about it. Because I intend to know!'

As she still remained silent, wondering what to tell him, wondering if he would believe the steps story—his voice, returning to that frightening tone he had used since they met this evening, said, 'You will either tell me, or we'll start again on what we were doing before I found out about all this. In fact . . .' His tone departed from the one of menace, and went soft, silken, as he repeated, 'In fact, that's what I would much rather be doing, believe me, so . . .'

Glancing up at that implacable face, Clarissa knew he would do as he said, so she looked past his shoulder, as he sat at her side on the bed, and said, 'If I tell you—all of it, can I go? Because it's true what I said. I really don't want to have anything more to do with you, Alexis.'

'We'll see,' was the reply she received—from a face which, like that in the car, was half in shadow, half in blinding light.

So she said, 'I fell out of a car!' There, let him make what he could out of that.

'You fell out of a car? No one falls out of a car these days, with seat-belts compulsory—unless a crowd of youngsters were going joy-riding, and, my dear Clarissa, I don't think that that was the case. So shall we start again?'

'Very well.' She took a deep breath and began. 'You'd warned me about Federico, and when one Sunday he offered me a lift home, I refused . . .' She stopped at an impatient movement coming from the man sitting so close. She wished he would get up off the bed.

However, she continued, 'Oh, I refused charmingly. I chatted smilingly. No one could take umbrage because of it.'

'Yes, I've noticed your manners—and your good sense. That's why . . .' Alexis broke off.

Startled, her glance swung round to him. But he wasn't looking at her, so she continued, cutting out as much as she was able, 'Well, there was that dance arranged for after the fête.' She saw him nod, and thought he probably knew all about it, but he didn't know about the accident—that she was sure of. 'And Jim Henson was supposed to call for me, but he had some kind of a transport problem.' Again Alexis gave that small agreeing nod, but Clarissa plunged on, wanting to get it over with.

'So, probably mischievously, because as you know he normally doesn't do that kind of thing, Federico offered to come and collect me. I came out on to the veranda, thinking it was Jim. What could I do? It would have been impossible to say I'd changed my mind about going when I was already out there and dressed. And that damned Federico knew it. So I said, "Thank you, you're very kind," or words to that effect, and went.'

Clarissa paused for a long while, and the man beside her rose, to lean back against a heavy wardrobe behind him. He made no comment.

'I think,' she began again, 'that when he told me he was only taking me for a pre-dance drink at his home, that would have been all it amounted to—when I showed that that was all I intended it to be. But . . .' here she turned and looked fully at the lounging figure, 'what price the looks going around if I'd turned up at the dance a couple of hours late, after Federico had left to call for me?

'You've shown me tonight how it would have been, and you have more cause to know me. If I *had* gone, this scene here tonight would probably still have happened, but I would have had no hurt shoulder to prevent it reaching the conclusion you'd planned for it! I dislike you now, Alexis. I would have hated you then!'

'All right, go on,' was all he said. So, tiredly, sick of it all, Clarissa said, 'I undid my seat-belt as quietly as I could, pressed the door-handle and threw myself out.'

These words did bring a reaction. 'But you could have been killed!' came the exclamation.

'Well, I wasn't. Now can I go home?'

'What happened? Don't tell me that Fred just left you, because I know he wouldn't. We've known one another for always. He may have different ways regarding women—but that doesn't apply to young girls, unless those girls show him differently. So did he get you and bring you home? There's been no talk at all, and believe me, I've listened for it.'

'Oh, please!' she began, holding out an entreating hand. She didn't want to discuss it any more. But a voice said only,

'I want to know.'

'Very well, I picked myself up from the ditch I'd rolled into and hobbled down into the cane,' here she noticed an involuntary movement from Alexis, but carried on regardless, 'I moved along the edge until I heard the car door slam quite some distance away, then I went into it.

'Federico walked up and down, calling to me. He said not to be bloody stupid, that he'd take me home if I came out. I could hear him swearing. I knew by the sound of it that it was swearing—anyone would know! It sounded so violent, in whatever language he was using.'

'He'd be using Greek. Fred swears in Greek and makes love in Spanish.' These words came to her so matter-of-factly that it took a moment for her to understand them.

She swung round on that lounging figure who had

spoken so quietly. 'How dare you, Alexis? It wasn't a laughing matter. I was frightened out of my mind!'

'And you had a right to be frightened. If this bizarre thing had happened to me, I think I'd have murdered you. Can you imagine the sort of stories such an occurrence would give rise to in a small town like here—where everyone knows one another, or at least knows of them, if it had come out? A girl throwing herself out of a car! Heavens above!'

'I don't care now, I didn't care then. He should have taken me properly to the dance!'

'Yes, he should have. What happened next?'

'He got into his car and drove around searching for me. I got home by the back streets. It wasn't far.'

'Oh, no, I guess it wasn't far. Not with a dislocated collarbone and half the skin off your leg!'

'I didn't care about any of that. I just didn't want it known. Look, you've heard it all. I'm tired, so will you please take me home?'

There was an appeal in her voice. She heard it and straightened. Heavens, she would be crying soon if she didn't watch out!

But that tall figure, lounging there so indolently behind her, asked, 'How did it not get out? I simply don't believe it could be kept quiet.'

Clarissa drew a deep breath, wondering if this nightmare would ever end, wanting only to be in her own room, to be able to pull the blankets right up over her head.

But draggingly she told him, 'Eddie, Alice's fiancé, is up for a big promotion, and she didn't want any scandal to touch him even remotely through her. So she cut off my ripped dress and called the doctor. By the time he arrived I was cleaned up and we'd come up with a story that I'd slipped on the stairs and grazed my leg on the wooden treads as I fell down them.'

'I can imagine him believing that!'

'For heaven's sake, Alexis, will you stop? He might not have, but it was a perfectly valid explanation. And we were two respectable girls in our own home, so what else could he do? That finally is the lot . . . Oh, no. Federico came as soon as the doctor left. I think that even Alice was a bit scared by the way he looked. But when we told him the story we'd concocted, he said he'd go back to the dance and be impatient about me—which he did very competently, so Sarah informed us. Now, that *is* the absolute lot! So I'm going home.'

Alexis went to put a hand on her arm, and suddenly she could stand no more. Cringing away from it, her body curling itself up into a tight ball, she told herself, I'm not going to cry, I'm not . . . but she couldn't prevent the racking sobs that shook her.

CHAPTER ELEVEN

SOMEWHERE outside her Clarissa knew that Alexis had left, that the room was empty. She hadn't heard him going, but then he always walked as silently as that stalking animal that decorated his car. She didn't care. All she was trying to do was stop those distressing sobs she had never meant to allow to happen. But so much had occurred in this last week, so much . . .

Alexis' voice said, 'Sit up and drink this, Clarissa,' and made to put his arm around her to help. Without thought, without conscious effort, cringing from that arm, her body rolled over and she was standing on the far side of the bed, and through tear-drenched eyes she gazed across the space between them.

'I've only brought you some brandy—you need it. You've been through a great deal of strain.' Alexis began to walk round the bed to her side.

Angrily, involuntarily, she backed away.

'Don't be silly. Just take it and drink it.'

The voice didn't hold the vibrant anger which had coloured Federico's when he had said those same words, but, gazing at him, Clarissa saw that his face held none of the charm or smiling amiability which was so often upon it. As it had appeared to her in the car, it again looked as if carved from granite, the lines about those sculptured lips deeply indented. And the eyes, half hooded, looked black, not grey. He reached out to her the hand holding the glass.

She said, 'I don't want it.'

'Whether you want it or not, drink it, or I promise you . . .' He didn't finish the sentence; he had no need to. So knowing that in the end she would have to, she put the glass of amber liquid to her mouth and sipped. Then she lowered it.

'All of it,' said that implacable voice.

She wondered what would happen if she threw it at him, and she shivered. She said, 'All right, I'll drink it, but then I'm going—if I have to start walking . . .' She paused, then added bitterly, 'And doing that won't be an unheard-of exercise in my young life!'

If anything, that face before her settled into deeper lines, but all he answered was, 'Finish it.'

So Clarissa upended the small glass and swallowed quickly. She coughed and spluttered, then backed away sharply, warding Alexis off as he moved towards her. Taking a deep breath to bring her breathing back to normal, she placed the glass on the night table beside the bed, held on to the piece of heavy furniture for support, and began, 'Look, Alexis . . .' She paused for quite some few seconds, and while he also remained silent, she remembered all the times she had actually said his name, thought of it, and even dreamed about it. But now, this time, she had spoken it with an entirely new inflection. She said again, 'Look, Alexis, I'll say it now because it doesn't matter any more. But you were always somewhere in the background of my life, from when I was seventeen. I used to tell myself that it was only a schoolgirl crush. But behind all my growing up, the image of a holiday up here and what happened during it cast its long shadow. I remembered riding magically on a windsurfer, I remembered being kissed on a river bank as darkness began to fall . . .'

She stopped for a moment as the man before her shifted involuntarily, then put up a hand to prevent him speaking. 'Oh,' she began again, 'I knew it wasn't for me that those kisses were meant; I knew something had happened to cause them. Still, your image remained as a magic memory!

'But now, if at any time I do accidentally come into

contact with you, that romantic illusion will have disappeared. I'll see the way you looked at me a minute ago; I'll hear the words you spoke to me, and also I'll remember that but for my hurt shoulder this evening would have finished in a very different manner. So I do have something to thank Federico for, although he'll never know it—a freedom to go out and begin an existence unencumbered by long-ago memories. Now . . .'

Before she could say again that she wanted to go home, Alexis said so softly that she had to listen intently, 'Very well, Clarissa, I'll take you home, but first, I'm not going to offer any apologies for tonight. I thought I had reason enough. And you know, you're not the only one who might have memories.

'However, before you go, I expect it's out of the question to offer you a meal? No, I didn't think so,' he added as she moved involuntarily away. He did continue speaking, however; he said, 'Your face might need a touch of make-up before you go out to see the gay metropolis on a Friday night, so would you like to use my bathroom?

'No,' he again said, as she made that involuntary movement for a second time. 'Well, there's a bathroom along the hallway which you already know . . . Good,' he finished as she nodded, and moved towards the door he had kicked shut such a little time ago.

He moved through it and stood aside, allowing her plenty of room to move past him. And in that familiar bathroom Clarissa splashed her face again and again with cold water, patted it dry, then, lipsticked and hair combed, she left.

Alexis was standing further along the corridor, leaning indolently—as she had so often seen him do—against the wall of it. He straightened when she appeared. He didn't speak; he only waited. He also kept silent on the drive home. But Clarissa said, 'You have no need to go right to the house, you can drop me on that corner.'

'My dear Miss Raymond, you were speaking about long years gone by, a short time ago. So I beg leave to inform you that long years have also passed since I left a girl I'd taken out down at the corner of the street. Nowadays I always drive right up.

'And I'm sure——' Something in the tone he was using made Clarissa glance directly at him. At that familiar face which had remained so impersonal since the aftermath of the love-scene in his bedroom. He was repeating, 'And I'm sure you'll be quite capable of coming up with some sort of story as to why Alexis Markham is driving you home!'

'Why, you . . .' Suddenly the calm with which she had been enveloped spun away, and she was violently angry. She finished unzipping her seat-belt, opened the door first, then turned to face him.

'Do you know, Alexis Markham, that after that distasteful episode of such a short time ago, I knew that if I *had* to come into contact with you, I could do it with complete indifference. But now I find I dislike you very much. I could almost say I hate you! I hope I never have to see you again!'

She didn't say goodbye. She stepped from the Jaguar, leaving the door swinging wide, went up the path, up the steps, took out her key to slide in the lock. All the time she could feel her shoulders cringing, aware that his gaze would be following her. Because he was who he was, she knew he would not drive away until she had gone inside.

But she wasn't aware of the expression his face held as he gazed after the hurrying figure. The dark countenance held a smile of satisfaction which widened as if some idea or thought had come to lodge within his mind.

Inside, Clarissa sagged against the door. Then, making an effort, she went through the lounge, quite able to see with the veranda light shining through. But in her own room, she dropped on to the straight-backed chair, her big shoulder-bag falling to the floor. And abruptly she felt the furious, violent anger dissipate.

Exhaustion was all she felt now. It had been too much, all that had happened—last week and then tonight. What had made Alexis behave as he had? He had certainly not made any commitment himself. And if she had gone out with Federico, well, too bad.

Oh, well . . . She would have to make the effort to rise up on legs which seemed to have no strength at all. Discarding the idea of a shower, Alexis' kisses on her or not, she undressed slowly and dropped a long nightdress over her head. She was to have the dressings off on Monday, but in the meantime, she didn't want Sarah's inquisitive eyes on their extensiveness.

Would she go and make something to eat? No, she felt as if she would never eat again. But she made herself walk—even if it was with dragging footsteps—out to the kitchen. She made tea and toast. She drank two cups of tea, tried to eat some toast, but found neither throat nor stomach would accept.

Back in her own room, she opened a small drawer in her dressing table, shook out two aspirins, then, with a shrug, added a third. They might help a little, and all she wanted was oblivion. So, swallowing them, she flicked out the light and climbed into bed.

She didn't expect to sleep. She expected that scene in Alexis' bedroom to go round and round in her mind. Alexis' image *was* there—but it remained only on the periphery of her vision. And little by little, in nature's way of taking care of its own, she sank deeply down into a sea of unconsciousness.

When she next surfaced to the world about her, she moved slowly, lethargy still enfolding her. Glancing at the window, she saw that it didn't appear early and wondered why there was no sound of the others being up. She turned to look at her bedside clock and saw that it was past seven. A furrow came between her brows, before the thought came that of course it was Saturday . . . when abruptly, shatteringly, remembrance of last night's happenings swamped through her.

The remembrance of Alexis' body lengthwise against her own, the remembrance of his fingers trailing her bare skin, the remembrance of his kisses . . . Clarissa moved restlessly. She knew that previously she had always gone into Alexis' embrace gladly, with happiness. Now she would only ever remember the way he had looked, the way he had acted because he had thought of her as he had.

Still, she was out from under his shadow now. Before, after being with him, he had always remained to colour her dreams. However, last night his image had been there, but it had been far away in the distance. So now she had to set about finding a new kind of life.

Thinking she had better begin, Clarissa swung out of bed. She prepared tea and toast, then deciding she had better eat, boiled two eggs. She was eating them when Alice came through the doorway. 'You're up early,' she said.

'No, not really, it's going on eight. I was just sitting here wondering what to buy for us to eat next week. It's my turn to feed us all then, you know. Would a roast do for tomorrow's dinner?'

'Just what the doctor ordered,' interrupted a new voice, and Sarah added from the doorway, 'I love your roasts, Clarissa.' She walked in, looked into the tea-pot, found it empty, and made herself a cup of coffee. 'Look——' she went on, then hesitated for a moment.

The other two girls glanced quickly at her. Sarah wasn't noted for a reluctance to have her say.

Both said, 'What do you want, Sarah?'

The redheaded girl laughed, then replied, 'I wondered

if we could ask Phil to come for dinner?'

'Who's Phil?' It was Clarissa who spoke this time.

'Oh, come on. You both know who Phil is!'

'I suppose he's your dishy policeman—but Sarah,' it was Clarissa again, 'about dinner. I don't know.'

'But why not?' chimed in Alice. 'I'll ask Eddie as well. Can you get a roast big enough for five—or six, if you want to ask anyone, Clarissa.'

'I expect I could buy a roast big enough. I don't know if I could cook it, though—and all that goes with it. I've only cooked for two at home, and three here—but why not? And no, I don't want to invite anyone,' Clarissa answered Alice's raised eyebrow.

'OK, then look.' No sign of hesitation coloured Sarah's attitude now, as she said, 'If you two go shopping, I'll clean up the kitchen and the bathroom. Now you can't ask for better than that.'

'Good heavens! We accept, but are you sure, my child, that you're feeling quite well?' asked Alice sarcastically.

And later, dressed in jeans and a long-sleeved check shirt—because somehow she felt that today she wanted to wear no voile or see-through silk—Clarissa walked past the kitchen to wait for Alice at the front door. She grinned at the busy girl within.

And it was also later, as she waited at the check-out counter with Alice, that she said a little anxiously, 'I've certainly spent up today, haven't I? A little extravagantly too, but still . . .' She spared a complacent look at the plump sirloin roast sitting among all the other groceries—which included truffles and handmade chocolates for after-dinner coffee. Her friend only smiled at her.

They paid for their goods, had them packed in two large packets, and, picking up hers, smiling over a shoulder at a remark Alice had made, Clarissa turned—to look directly into a tanned, handsome face, into smiling slate-grey eyes.

For a second she stopped dead in her tracks at this unexpected appearance, but she quickly recovered to send her gaze staring blankly over his shoulder. However, Alexis was speaking to her companion even as he reached out to take the large carton from Clarissa.

'Someone told me,' he was saying, 'that Clarissa has hurt her shoulder. Should she be carrying a heavy parcel like this?'

Two voices spoke at once. 'There's nothing wrong with me. Of course I can carry it,' said one.

'Oh, heavens!' The other tone was stricken. 'Of course you probably shouldn't, Clarissa. I just didn't think.'

Relieved of her large parcel, Clarissa began to stalk away, because that was the only way the manner of her departure could be described. But Alexis was speaking pleasantly, casually, as they strolled along the wide footpath and turned a corner to where their car was parked.

Packages deposited inside, he turned to look at both girls, Alice with a smiling face, Clarissa with a stony one that still gazed past his shoulder. He lifted a wrist to glance at his watch. 'Look,' he told them, 'I have an appointment with my accountant at noon. I was just thinking about a cup of coffee. Take pity on a lonely man, and join me.'

Before Clarissa could interject to say she didn't drink coffee, that pleasant, easy voice pre-empted her. 'Or a cup of tea if you prefer it.'

Angrily, her gaze did now swing to him. She knew that last sentence had been directed at her. He knew she preferred tea. However, he met her furious look with a blandness across his entire face.

Alice was looking at her, wondering at her attitude. Then Alexis said, 'You can then tell me about the position your fiancé is in line for, Alice. I think you might be getting some good news soon.'

Of course that did it, thought Clarissa vindictively, whether Alexis knew anything about it or not. Then fairness brought her angry thoughts up short. Of course he would not say—or even intimate—something that he knew might not be true.

So perforce she walked beside them as they went across to the café, sat stiffly in the chair he pulled out for her, and decided to just sit out the time until they left.

Ordering whatever it was he was ordering, Alexis turned to Alice. And apparently he did know about the job Eddie was applying for, because that topic occupied them until the coffee—and a teapot—came along. Also arriving were the cream-filled pastries and cakes this place was noted for.

Clarissa didn't even have to pour her own tea. Her host did it for her. And he might put a cream- and nut-filled case of puff pastry on her plate, but she didn't have to eat it—and she didn't!

She did catch the puzzled glance Alice was sending in her direction, and decided that a show of good manners was called for, so she sat with a cup in both hands, drinking slowly.

Her gaze out on the busy thronged street was suddenly obscured. She looked up. Two nurses in their white uniforms, red shoulder capes fastened at the throat, but slung back, had come to stand between her and the outside view she had been looking at.

'Hi, there, lovely to see you again so soon, Mr Markham,' said one.

Alexis had risen. He smiled and said, 'Yes, it was only yesterday at the hospital. Are you off to begin work at once, or can you join us in a cup of coffee?'

'Oh, no, we're going off duty, but we'd love some

coffee, wouldn't we, Jenny?' exclaimed the one who had greeted Alexis.

They were soon introduced and settled. Coffee and more cakes arrived. And if Clarissa wasn't sending her smiles and attention towards their host, the two newcomers certainly were! Well, they could have him, she thought, her glance under downcast lashes seeing the so obvious laughing invitations he was receiving.

She looked at her watch, and intercepting that glance, Alice said, 'I think we'd better be on our way, Alexis. It would be a good idea to get our groceries out of the car and into the fridge. Thank you so much for the coffee.' She rose, smiling goodbye at the nurses.

Before Clarissa could rise herself, Alexis had stood and walked casually round. He took hold of her chair to bring it back, and unexpectedly, out of the blue, the fingers of both hands resting against her shoulders sent shock-waves threading her system. She rose quickly, almost stumbling, and they were looking directly at one another. They stood, both of them, immobile for the space of a heartbeat, held together by a stretched cord of tension, then Clarissa had turned and walked blindly out.

But she could still feel the area where his fingers had touched—as if an open flame had sent its scorching heat to brand her. Hailed by a colleague from her own school, Alice turned smilingly to speak to him.

Thankfully finding she was on her own for a few precious seconds, Clarissa shook her head to clear it. And, focusing properly now, she looked out on a blue and golden landscape, brilliant with the warmth and sunlight of a tropical day; at this small town she had come to like so much. What had happened back there? Last night she had been so confident that she was free of Alexis. But now—her lips twisted in a derisive smile—she knew that if she didn't avoid him, deliberately keep away from any vicinity he could be in, he would only have to beckon and she would follow.

Alexis was her reason for existing. And she knew that was how it would always be—whatever she did, wherever she went to live her life. So it was still almost blindly that she fell into step when Alice hurried to rejoin her. And she must have spoken and acted normally, because she was subjected to no more puzzled glances.

In the garage they were collecting their shopping when Sarah ran down the front steps to help them. 'What do you want now?' asked Alice ironically.

'Well, actually I don't want anything.' Sarah was walking upstairs with one of the large packages. Turning on entering the lounge, she said, 'However, I rang Phil to invite him to lunch tomorrow, and . . . and he asked would we care to have one of his flatmates to come along and partner Clarissa. I said I'd ring back. But it *would* be nice to have an even number, wouldn't it? And Phil says he's very nice.'

Unable to help herself, suddenly Clarissa was doubled up, lacking the power to stop the half-hysterical laughter welling out. Even numbers, no less! He was very nice, no less. When she was head over heels, fathoms deep, in love with the most handsome and attractive man she had ever known or seen—and that included Federico.

She made herself stop, and straightened up. Throwing out her arms, she said unsteadily, 'OK, Sarah, be my guest and organise to your heart's content.'

CHAPTER TWELVE

CLARISSA stood by the open door of the bus waiting for her class. It came along, some of the children dawdling, others skipping along excitedly. She hadn't wanted to take this outing, and had said so to her boss. 'But a sugar mill—the kids will know all about it!'

'Oh, no, they won't. Only half of them belong to the town; the other half to children of the parents who serve it and are only here on transfer. And they all should see how sugar is crushed, even the ones who belong here, because sugar is the life-blood of this community, so they should be made aware of that.'

So here was Clarissa counting them as they trod the high steps. Fourteen—she could manage them, but she caught hold of young Billy, whom she knew from past experience. He squirmed and said, 'I wasn't doing anything, miss.'

'No, you weren't, and you're not going to either. You will sit in front, just behind the driver, where I can see you.'

'Aw . . . miss!'

Taking no notice of the unhappy plea those two words carried, she said to their driver, 'That's the lot, and may the Lord have mercy upon me!'

He just grinned, and sent the big vehicle on its journey. At the mill, he pulled into a parking space, from where the whole vast structure appeared monstrous. Clarissa remembered passing it when it had been deserted and silent. It wasn't silent today. So, reading the riot act in her nastiest voice, she descended the steps and waited on the tarmac for the children to gather round. They were to be met, she knew, and, glancing about, she was thankful to see a man dressed in white shirt and fawn slacks coming towards them. He was their guide, and she found to her surprise that as he explained the processes, the children were actually interested.

And so was she, until he raised a hand in greeting to someone beyond their small group. Clarissa looked casually to see who it was, and gazed into Alexis' eyes. Why was he here? she thought furiously. He had no right to be in evidence everywhere she went! But, turning away, she grinned wryly, common sense asserting itself. This mill was probably the one that crushed his cane.

He had joined their guide, speaking to him as they progressed to a new area. She walked behind the children, keeping them in her vision, edging around to watch them. A voice called sharply, 'Look out, Clarissa!' and a hand came out to grasp her arm.

She spun round. She hadn't seen the big machine behind her. The guide said soothingly, 'It's all right, Alexis, there was no danger. Miss Raymond was watching the children, but I was keeping an eye on where she was.' He only smiled as she glanced behind to see huge knives in a huge machine that was chopping the cane-stalks to fragments. Heavens! She shuddered—she had had no idea.

Her arm released, Alexis spoke a few more words with their guide and, raising a hand in farewell, departed. But his presence had disrupted her concentration. She made herself pay attention, because it *was* fascinating, this method of taking what were merely thick stalks of green foliage, progressing from one process to another, to have it all come out in a mountain of raw brown sugar. The refining was done elsewhere.

She said to the man who had told her, 'Call me Steve,' 'You know, I'll never take another spoonful of sugar without thinking of green cane and a monstrous mill that crushes it.'

At the finishing line, they were trooped out of the vast, echoing building to a room where bottles of fruit juice and coloured milk were handed out. Clarissa was told smugly when she protested that it was an exercise in good will.

She did say when the moment came to leave, 'Should I go and thank anyone—the manager, or someone?'

'Good heavens, no!' Two arms were flung up in horror. 'I'm afraid he wouldn't appreciate your lot going into his holy of holies. But still,' a flashing smile was sent her way, 'I'll pass on your thanks; and speaking of thanks for a job well done, have you a telephone number?'

'Well, actually,' she smiled at him, and for the first time up here fell into the old act of mild flirtation she had been so good at; that practised art of keeping an interested male friendly, but without any commitment on her side, 'Well, actually,' she repeated, 'I'm afraid I don't have a telephone number that's available. I'm only a poor working girl, you know . . . Hey you, you come here!' The last words were not addressed to Steve but to Billy, for whom she had made a dash. Collecting him and then hustling him up the steps, she turned and sent a brilliant, radiant smile at Steve, then, seeing all her charges were on board, joined them.

She didn't see a tall, familiar figure emerge from the administration building further along, coming out of what her guide of this afternoon had called the 'holy of holies', and who was accompanied by the mill manager himself. She didn't see him, either, intercept that brilliant smile which was so seldom in evidence, as she sent it to the man seeing them off, or the scrutiny that that same man was being subjected to.

On the drive home, with only a teacher's absent ear tuned in to the chatter going on all around, Clarissa looked out of her window, again thinking absently that when this land up here turned on its tropical fine weather, it certainly did! The arch above was a deep blue sapphire, its sunshine a golden yellow warmth that touched everything.

Remembering Steve—deliberately not remembering another face—she decided that at least *he* had been interested in her, and so had that policeman, that detective, whom Phil had brought along for dinner.

She was suddenly, blindingly envious of Sarah's bubbling pleasure, knowing she had never experienced that unalloyed, casually searched-after happiness that was the lot of most girls. Scorching, demanding kisses on a darkening river bank when she was so young had wiped away any of that! There had been no need to search! She had always known that, from that very time.

She drew a deep breath, thinking wryly as the bus pulled into the school yard, oh, well, back to the saltmines! She settled the class down, told them she expected a story all about their trip to a sugar mill on her table by Monday morning. She ignored their 'Aw, miss!' and, finishing the day, she dismissed them.

Sauntering home, she thought of the weekend starting tomorrow, and their excursion down to the beach on Sunday. She could go swimming—providing she was careful about the scars on her leg. She glanced in the letterbox in passing. No mail. But Sarah was home and called out, 'A letter from your mother, Clarissa. On the hall table.'

None, of course, with black, dashing script, and she dismissed the image of the writer of it whom she had seen just this afternoon, but without thought, without volition, her fingers came up to clasp the place where other fingers had rested so tightly, only an hour or so ago.

She walked into the kitchen, opening her letter, giving a shake of her head to Sarah's, 'I'm making coffee, I don't expect you'd like a cup,' then glanced up with a smile when Sarah sat a glass of fruit juice tinkling with ice down before her.

Sipping it, she said, 'Mum's got a job working in a big tourist complex selling souvenirs of Darwin and the Northern Territory. She says she loves it. Isn't that marvellous?'

They drank their juice and coffee, idly talking—Clarissa of her afternoon's visit to the mill, Sarah about an incident which had caused a minor row at school. Clarissa didn't mention a word about another individual she had come into contact with that afternoon. She rose after a while, saying, 'I'm going to change and then come out to prepare dinner. But tomorrow is my last day, then you take over on Sunday, my friend,' she smugly reminded her companion.

'Don't I know it! But still, I can tell you I think I'm quite clever. On Sunday we're having the day at the beach, and anything goes for meals then. And next Friday night,' Sarah added laughingly, 'we're all invited out to dinner by Phil and Kent, to say thank you for the meal here. Actually,' she laughed again across at Clarissa, 'it was suggested for tonight, but I put it off until next Friday. After all, you're cook for tonight, and next Friday it's me, so . . .'

It was Clarissa who laughed now, but she only said as she departed for the bedroom, 'Time will catch up with you one day, my girl!'

The week that followed was easy, restful. Clarissa put on a machine-full of clothes the next day, and also did some hand-washing, pressed a few light winter garments she unearthed from the bottom of her large case, and met the other two downstairs as Sarah had done when they had returned from shopping, but with no suggestion or invitations to offer.

They watched TV after dinner, then went down to the beach on Sunday, where Clarissa thoroughly enjoyed herself. She swam and sunbathed, played ball on the hot white sand, but watched carefully that the rapidly fading scar on her leg had sunscreen over it at all times. She also saw a great many windsurfers. But not the one she kept a wary eye out for.

They went to see a new James Bond movie on Wednesday night, and then of course to dinner on Friday. They didn't go to the exclusive restaurant to which Alexis had taken her, but she enjoyed herself. They ate seafood, talked of the state of the world, about their own sugar, about films, and were joined by Jerry and his girlfriend, to help the laughter along.

It was going on for eleven when, as they congregated outside on the footpath, Jerry and his girl departing, Alice and Eddie waving goodbye, that Phil suggested a drive down to the beach. Clarissa looked at Kent. She said carefully, 'Could I have a rain-check? As Sarah knows, I had a small accident a little while ago, and now that virus which is going round seems to have caught up with me. I really wouldn't like to continue on. It *is* a little late.'

Beginning to interrupt hotly, Sarah was silenced. Kent said, 'That's fine. I'll give you that rain-check, but don't think, Clarissa, that I won't be around to collect it. OK?'

And so it was. Clarissa sat in the back seat, and beside her Kent talked casually. He said yes, in answer to a question from her, that he liked this town, but it was only a stepping stone. He walked up the front steps with her, and under the veranda light stood gazing quizzically down. She thought suddenly, panicking, I couldn't bear it!

Some of her reluctance must have surfaced. Kent had been going to kiss her goodnight—the intention was there on his face. However, he now just took her hand and said quietly, 'I'll be in touch about that rain-check. Goodnight.' He had turned to run lightly down the steps and out to the waiting car.

Sinking down on her bed once she was inside, Clarissa knew fatalistically that what she had felt out there on the veranda would always be there. She knew now that she would have to make sure that there would be no rain-check collected. Even the mere thought of being kissed by another man than Alexis sent revulsion through her entire being. She would be cooking no more dinners—nor be going out among masculine company who might be interested in her.

She played tennis at the school on Sunday; but it was on Monday evening that she was informed of a happening which was to bring in its train an altogether different attitude to her behaviour.

Clarissa was writing a letter to her mother on the dining-room table; Sarah was doing hand-washing in the laundry, coming back and forth to talk. Observing the shadows falling across her paper, Clarissa glanced at her wrist watch. Alice was late.

Letter finished, she said to Sarah who had also finished her chores and had come inside, 'I hope nothing has happened. It's after six o'clock. Alice is awfully late . . . I'd go and start dinner except for the fact that I don't know what she's decided on.'

'Oh, she may have been kept at school, or be with Eddie. It won't matter tonight if we eat late. No one is going out.'

'No, I don't suppose it will.' But a furrow had come to lodge between Clarissa's brows, then as suddenly had cleared away. They had both heard the car drive into the garage. Then Alice was standing in the doorway.

She looked at the two girls, and then staid, placid Alice had rushed across and with her arms around them both, was dancing up and down, saying, 'We've got it! Eddie's got it!'

'Oh, the job? Isn't that marvellous? I'm so glad for you both.' Clarissa hugged her back. Sarah said, 'That's fantastic! Come sit down and tell us all about it.' They were being told all about it, when suddenly Sarah broke in miserably,

'Oh, heavens, you'll be leaving, and we'll have someone else pushed here upon us. Oh, well,' here she grinned widely over at Clarissa, and added, 'we'll be two to one, so she'd better co-operate!'

Clarissa only smiled carefully in reply. She thought, I'm sorry, Sarah, but you'll be breaking in two new girls. I won't be here either. Then her thoughts were brought abruptly back to the present when Alice said, 'We were at the hospital when Alexis and Lesley came along. They congratulated Eddie, and Alexis said we'd have to celebrate the occasion, that he had a friend with a big launch and how about all of us sailing through the Hinchenbrook Channel and among the islands one weekend?'

'Oh, truly, Alice? Lucky you! You'll have a fantastic time with Alexis arranging it,' came from Sarah.

'You too, Sarah. We're all invited.'

Clarissa remained silent, while Sarah said, 'But what about Phil? I don't want to go without him.'

'Well . . .' Alice laughed, 'Alexis didn't especially mention Phil. He did say, however, that you could invite your current boyfriend. He didn't say you could, Clarissa, so I expect he's making up a party.' She glanced at Clarissa a little anxiously, no doubt remembering a conversation on a morning not so long ago.

Clarissa's first thought had been to refuse, then her second one was, what the hell? I'm leaving here at the year's end and most likely will never come back, so it would be nice to see and cruise among those fabled islands. So she said with a laugh, 'Well it's something that I should be needed to make up a party's numbers!'

The presence of Alexis over the next three weeks was only remarkable by its absence. She did get a letter written in that dashing black script, but then so did Alice

and Sarah. It was an invitation to a weekend to
sail among the islands, with an overnight stay at Dunk
Island.

'Good heavens—Dunk Island!' The exclamation came
almost simultaneously from her two companions as they
all opened and read their letters. Then, from Sarah,
'We'd never be able to afford it. It's an expensive
playground for the wealthy. Some Lord or someone
opened it, but then the war came and it had to be
abandoned. One of the big airlines has it now. Oh!' Sarah
kissed her letter and swung around dancing. 'Oh, lovely,
lovely weekend!'

Clarissa knew that she couldn't kiss *her* letter,
but she could store it away carefully with the other two
which had been written by the same hand. And she
did.

Then, as it was the mid-term holiday break, Sarah
went home and took Clarissa with her for a weekend.
Alice and Eddie went to look around Cairns for that same
weekend. Back again, they went shopping. And as far as
Clarissa was concerned, it was very careful shopping. She
had every intention of being turned out as exquisitely as
any other guest who might be among the passengers . . .
Mrs Thornton, Lesley, or whoever.

She finally chose a pair of fine pink cotton slacks with a
knitted overblouse in the same colour. Then shorts and
top in her favourite colour of lemon yellow—not at all the
same shade of a dress that she had had once sent to her.
And of course she knew she wouldn't have to buy a frock
for dining and dancing at this place the other girls called
'fabulous Dunk Island'. Her white Grecian gown would
do very well.

Time seemed funny to her around that period. One
minute it appeared to be dragging, the days seemingly
never-ending. The next, they were flying on wings she
didn't know if she wanted to go fast or slow.

Then finally time passed, as it always does, whether

wanted to or not, and they were waiting in the lounge to
be called for. Alexis didn't play the polite gentleman and
come up for them. He merely tooted the horn. But he was
outside the big car, waiting beside the open back door,
when they arrived. Phil leaned over from his seat in the
front, saying, 'Hello, beautiful,' and, glancing at the
redheaded girl, Clarissa saw a tinge of colour stain her
cheeks. She had never seen Sarah disconcerted before, so
things must be serious, she thought.

And that thought caused her to glance upwards at
Alexis, and she stood immobile, suddenly unable to force
her body to move. He hadn't been expecting that quick
look and she had seen the expression his eyes contained.
Again it was as if a cord of invisible steel held them
together, then he moved, and Clarissa found herself
inside. The door slammed shut, the driver moving
around the back of the Jaguar to slip behind the wheel.
She heard the slam of his door. She had never experienced
the closing of this car's doors in such a fashion
before.

Driving quickly out through town and then off the
main highway on to a gravelled byroad, they soon had a
sea of olive and emerald green on both sides hemming
them in. There was a vehicle ahead that they were
following as it twisted and turned on the narrow track.
Alexis was saying, 'Your co-host for today is a bloke
called Frank, a bachelor who farms a large acreage, but
has only one love—his boat. He'd do better to put as
much time into his cane.' The words were said easily with
no trace of condemnation, but Clarissa grinned, thinking,
there speaks the farmer!

Alexis was continuing, 'We all try to remedy his
shortcomings about that—and he takes us sailing;
it's called fair exchange. You'll like him—everyone
does.'

The car before them had pulled to a stop on a cleared
river bank, and the Jaguar had come to a halt alongside it.

Lesley Armitage stepped out. 'That's the new doctor from the hospital,' whispered Alice of the man who had come to stand beside her, 'and Stella Martin, a Sister, also from there,' she added softly before going to meet Eddie, who had driven down with them.

Alexis was suddenly smiling down at Clarissa. 'As everyone else seems to have deserted you,' he said, throwing out a hand to exclaiming passengers who were busy greeting others, 'I expect I'll have to look after you, if you'll permit. Come along and meet your host.'

And, walking with him towards the small group congregated before a sleek, gleaming, big white launch tied up there, Clarissa received a further shock.

Standing beside a petite pretty stranger was a man who was no stranger at all. He said, 'Hi there, Clarissa. Nice to see you again.' And once more, without her meaning it to, her glance swung to Alexis. Except that he was holding her elbow, he was paying her no attention as he greeted the hospital contingent. So Clarissa met those smiling, remembering tawny eyes, with blue ones holding only polite blankness, and told him,

'And it's nice to see you too, Federico. When *was* the last time we met?'

He only laughed, and before he could reply Alexis was beside him. He said, 'Have you introduced Sophia yet, Fred? And Frank?'

'No. I haven't had time. Clarissa and I were just trying to remember when we last met. But it couldn't have been important, because we can't recall it. This is Sophia, Clarissa, up here from Sydney, and we hope to give her a weekend she'll always remember.'

Clarissa smiled at the pretty youngster opposite, saying, 'I'm happy to meet you, Sophia, and I hope that I too will have a weekend that I'll always remember.'

'Oh, yes. And I'm happy to meet you to. You're a schoolteacher, Federico told me. You don't look like one.' She was looking Clarissa over in her lovely pink slacks, her form-fitting pink top, the long fair pageboy-bobbed hair swinging shining and eye-catching about her shoulders.

Clarissa knew that a faint colour had come to stain her cheeks, even though the admiring words had been spoken with only friendliness, and involuntarily her glance was drawn to the two men, both now standing behind Sophia, one tall and handsome, bronzed as dark as the shorter, broader one, if in a different shade. Both dressed in pristine white shorts and silk shirts, and both were looking at her in perfect amity.

She gritted her teeth and thought, wouldn't I like to push you—both of you—backwards into that river behind you, and just stay here and watch a crocodile come and eat you up!

Then abruptly people had moved, then coalesced again, and she was being introduced to Frank, who had handed the other feminine guests up the gangway. She felt her hand taken in a hard, callused one; she saw the flash of white in a dark mahogany-hued face, as he told her, 'You make Alexis look after you, now. He's inclined to only enjoy himself, and leave the work to others.'

'Praise the Lord in heaven! Look who's talking!' came in shocked tones from Alexis behind her . . . close behind her. 'This from you, Frank, who does the least work a man can manage to do on his pathway through life!'

'Talk less, and throw off those mooring lines,' he was told. And as they all congregated upon the deck, forming into groups and pairs, Frank had stepped into the cockpit and taken the wheel. Then, without her being aware of it, Clarissa saw that the low, muddy banks on both sides were sliding past.

'Come along down and I'll show you where to put your cases,' said Alexis. And with laughing curiosity they stepped down into a small saloon, along an even smaller corridor off which opened two staterooms.

'This,' said Alexis, indicating one, 'is for you girls to change, or rest, or whatever. The other one is for the men, for the same purpose. Leave your luggage and then come up for drinks.'

They left their cases and followed him. But Clarissa was wondering who Sophia was. Who did she belong to? There had been no ring on her finger. But was she Federico's or Alexis's guest? Well, it wasn't going to be any of her business. She had vowed to herself that she was just going to be a tourist this weekend, and thoroughly enjoy herself.

She sat on the raised deck above the saloon and gazed out at the riverbanks. She didn't see any crocodiles, but soon there were only dense mangroves on either side, civilisation gone. A presence came to stand before her and said, 'Wine, Clarissa? Champagne, or just fruit juice?'

So, in the guise of a welcoming tourist, she smiled directly up at Alexis, and said, 'Perhaps champagne later. Fruit juice for now, thanks.'

She took her glass, and with Sophia and Stella and the new doctor, called Ray, sitting also on her seat, idly talked as they drank. Lesley stayed by Frank in the cockpit, and undoubtedly was interested in the boat and all its works. But it wasn't long before the smooth motion they had been enjoying changed, the launch going bumpily up and down. They were crossing the mouth of the river to emerge on to the ocean.

Carrying her glass, Clarissa moved to the front of the boat and leaned against the railings. Out from land now, the ocean below showed pure opaline colours, iridescent, changing. A smile curled her lips. What had someone said at Alexis's barbecue? Something about it being Alexis' lucky weather.

Well, he was lucky with today's. It was tourist-
brochure weather. A deep turquoise sky covered them;
golden sunshine gleamed on water that changed wherever
you looked, from deep, dark cobalt in the far distance,
shading into emerald green, and then to a lapis lazuli
where the wake of their passage parted it below. A cool
salt breeze caught at her swinging hair, sending it
dancing.

'Have you sailed at all, Clarissa?' asked Alexis, who
had come to stand at the rail. He was not crowding her,
but she felt the hard length of his body along her whole
side.

She said only, 'Yes, but only a little. Just an occasional
outing while I was at college. This is lovely, isn't
it?'

'Yes, it is today. However, it can get wild and woolly if
you're out in bad weather.'

'Have you ever been out in bad weather, Alexis?' And
because she was interested in the subject, she turned to
meet him, looking upwards.

He didn't answer at once as his gaze rested on her face.
Clarissa felt it as if her lips had been touched; she stayed
motionless, immobile, feeling the magnetism of that tall,
hard body reaching out to her, and she knew now
completely that all her decisions, the way she had thought
at times, didn't matter any more. If he wanted her, for
whatever reason, at whatever time, he would only have to
beckon. She would go to him . . . and then pay the price
asked.

Without meaning it to, her hand went out to him
entreatingly. It wasn't taken. And she heard the violent
expletive as he turned aside. Blindly she went to leave,
but Alexis caught hold of her, bringing her back to
him. He said now, 'Will you do something for me,
Clarissa?'

She went to say automatically, Of course, but then said

hesitantly, 'If I can!'

'Oh, you can if you will. You do realise that from the start we seem to have got off on the wrong foot? With the experience that I've accumulated over the years, you would think I could have managed things better. Still, that's water under the bridge now. So suppose we take this weekend as just a time to get to know one another, to enjoy a sun-filled holiday among friends, to laze and swim, and . . .' He reached out and took hold of her hand, then turned his fingers so that their two hands were entwined.

Clarissa looked down, at the long, tanned fingers among her shorter apricot ones, then turned her glance upwards. She found she couldn't say yes. She found she couldn't say anything. But her look said it all.

Alexis drew in a deep breath, held it for a heartbeat of time, then said, 'Yes, well, we'll start now, shall we?' And with his back towards the cockpit, hiding her standing before him, he lifted the entwined fingers to prise them open. He gazed down at her palm cupped in his hand, then bent his handsome head. She felt those firm, sculptured lips rest within it, moving gently back and forth. Then it was released and Alexis was strolling away.

Clarissa didn't move away. She turned back to stare blindly at the ocean, at the hazy lines of islands breaking its sapphire emptiness. She curled her hand into a tight fist. What was she to make of these last few moments? Alexis was no Federico. He wouldn't say . . . he wouldn't act as he had just done to make amusement for a holiday weekend.

So it was she now who took a deeply needed breath. She didn't have to change the thoughts she had set out with. She would still treat this outing as a holiday weekend. If it came with a bonus—and again her hand curled tightly into a protective fist over the moving kiss he had placed within it—she would swing free and accept what the gods provided.

Of course she took part in the happenings of the day; of course she was aware of what she was doing. But behind it all was a hazy brilliance of something she wouldn't allow herself to think of.

Later on she had come to sit, as the other girls were doing, in the shade of a canvas awning the men had erected. The boat on automatic control, even Lesley had deserted the cockpit and, beside Frank, was outstretched in the sun. A bikini became her, thought Clarissa, then decided a little maliciously that she herself had the better figure for them.

'I need this,' Lesley was saying, stretching voluptuously. 'And so does Ray here.' She poked a hand at the sunburnt figure of her workmate, who was also outstretched in the sun. 'I've been on night shift, and he's been on call with a broken night, so Alexis,' she had turned a lazy head to the figure who had just emerged from below with a tray full of mugs, 'we're going to just laze and sunbathe and be waited on.'

'Well, of course. Aren't you my guests? And behold, here's the start—morning tea. Fred and I have been busy. It's a little late, I'm afraid, but then lunch is going to be late too.' Alexis laughed across at Federico who was also clasping a tray, saying, 'You don't look as if doing this sort of thing is very familiar to you, Fred.'

'You're not wrong! But on being informed by one's host that a passage has to be worked for, what's a man to do?'

Drinking tea from a cup handed to her, suddenly Clarissa had lost interest in it. Alexis had finished his chores and had come to drop casually down on to the deck beside her. Not close, just entering the group in that position.

But it wasn't like the way Alexis had behaved up to now. His attitude to her in public had been distant and circumspect at all times. And here, under the awning, he could have sat anywhere, beside anyone, yet he had come to deliberately sit beside her.

Her head bent, she gazed down into her tea-mug, and thought that with just the tiniest of movements she could reach out a hand and touch that tanned thigh, even though of course she wouldn't. Why had he done this? she wondered, then shook her head at her own question. There was a weekend to enjoy—thoughts and wondering could wait until afterwards.

Alexis glanced round at his sitting, laughing, happily involved guests, and said with careful softness, 'And what do you think of Fred's intended?'

'Is she? I thought she might be! She seems a sweet little girl.'

'Yes, she is. And it will be a successful marriage, a very happy one. She's head over heels in love with him, and will defer to him in all his wishes. I can read your expression, Clarissa,' Alexis was continuing in that same tone of threaded silk, soft, sliding. 'Don't you think that what I've just told you is a happy state of affairs?'

Today seemed to be a different ball-game altogether, so she raised her face to him and said smilingly, 'I entirely agree that your first statement would indeed be a happy state of affairs, but I'm afraid I don't agree with your second.'

It was Alexis smiling widely at her now, and his next words were spoken so that they could only reach to where she was sitting. He said, 'Wouldn't you agree with all the wishes of the man you were to marry, Clarissa?'

Before she could reply, a voice called, 'Alexis, we're pretty close to that land. And I'm telling you it's not the sort of tropical island my imagination has conjured up. You know what I mean,' Ray threw out an all-encompassing hand, 'the one with swaying palms, creaming turquoise water lapping gently on silver sands . . . and of course, dusky, dancing maidens.'

'Oh, we'll come to them, Ray.' Alexis was laughing. 'That's the rocky side of one of the big islands in the Hinchinbrook Channel which we're cruising through now. But we'll be passing the ones of your dreams directly, and we'll be at Pelorus Islands soon, where we're having lunch. I promise you it will be all you imagined—except of course for the dusky, dancing maidens. But then you really can't expect paradise here on earth, can you?'

'Oh, I wouldn't say that. I can always expect . . .' Ray smilingly joined in the laughter that swelled up all around him.

CHAPTER THIRTEEN

AND LATER, in swimming gear, when they had arrived at the island Alexis had mentioned, Clarissa glanced about her, at this environment that *was* a paradise. Down beneath where the anchor had just slid with a heavy plop, the water didn't show the iridescent opaline shades of the deep ocean, but the clear light blue of aquamarine, the shimmering green of pale emerald, and the pellucid gentle colour of jade.

Clarissa drew a deep breath. To be able to come and be among all this, to walk on that beckoning silver sand, to swim . . . and to recline under those hundreds of swaying, whispering palms growing so high they almost obscured the cerulean arch above was something the gods had provided for them today. And if for her there was an added bonus, she would accept it, and let what came afterwards take care of itself.

'OK, here we go.' Alexis stood by the rail and gestured to the gangway of just a few steps, below which the phut-phut of an outboard engine was sending up its echoes. He told them, 'Fred and I will swim in. You lot will be a bit crowded, but it will only be for a few yards.'

As they phutted in, Clarissa smiled across at Ray and said, 'You really can't ask for the addition of dusky maidens. This,' an arm gestured around her, 'dredges up all the poetry one has ever read. Isn't there a saying about "see Naples and die"? Well, I'm telling everyone that nothing could outshine this!'

Ray only grinned back at her. 'As you say,' he answered, giving an assessing look at the girls

surrounding him, 'but you've missed a point. I
even have the dancing maidens—even if they're not
dusky.'

Lesley pushed him and he fell overboard into the
shallow, creaming waves. They had arrived, and the
small dinghy was grating on the shelving beach. Helped
out by Frank, two females turned automatically as a
laughing call echoed across from the launch. They were in
time to see two tanned bodies curve out and over to enter
the depths beneath, and then the same bodies cleave
towards them with effortless overarm strokes.

Frank wasn't looking at the swimmers; his hand up to
shade his eyes, he was gazing further out, and it was
Sarah, a Northener too, who said, 'Shouldn't they be
careful? This is shark territory, you know.'

'Yes, it is. And they do know—and they'll be careful.
But I'm telling all of you now. Enjoy your swim, but keep
in the shallows.'

Casual about his warning remarks, Frank then
indicated the cartons and coolers to Ray and Phil, and
strode before them up to the fringing edge of the swaying
palms. Joined by the swimmers before they reached the
circle of greenery which guarded the entire length of white
silver sand, they were ordered to discard their towels or
whatever and come and swim.

So, casually dropping her new jade green towelling
robe, to stand exposed in her also new green bikini,
Clarissa saw that she had been slow. The others, in pairs,
were all racing ahead, and with gleaming slate-grey eyes,
looking her over from head to foot, Alexis was reaching
out a tanned arm for her.

He gave her no time to think or dawdle. She found
herself racing along, her fingers clasped tightly in other
hard, compelling fingers. They were released at the
water's edge, and there, confused by these marked

attentions, she took a flat running dive into deeper water, erupting a short distance from them all.

But Alexis was there waiting for her when she emerged. He laughed across at her, saying, 'You look like a baby seal with your hair flattened like that! I've only seen you before—except for one remembered occasion—as if you'd just stepped from a beauty salon.'

He left her abruptly, to strike further out. Had he suddenly remembered that evening, that searing love-scene in the corridor hallway? Of course his words had brought it back; of course she was remembering it. Didn't she remember all the occasions with him? She slid down beneath the water.

When she came up she saw they were all staying in close to the beach. And, swimming around in the pale lapis-lazuli water, she decided that the day, the time, was magical.

She noticed that Frank wasn't swimming, but was phut-phutting back and forth beyond them all. Even as she looked, Lesley had shouted to him and was scrambling up into the small dinghy. Then Clarissa wasn't noting anything or anyone else. Alexis was beside her again, and there he stayed for the rest of the time they swam.

As she floated haphazardly, her glance on the turquoise arch above, hearing Alexis speaking yards, and sometimes only inches away, she thought, this is happiness.

Sarah, whose skin burnt so easily, was the first to say reluctantly that she had better get out, and Stella agreed, saying, 'Yes, me too.'

Sophia was just beyond, Federico remaining beside her. *She*, thought Clarissa a trifle enviously, didn't need to worry about sunburn, having that lovely matt olive skin. However, she also said, as reluctantly as Sarah had done,

'I think I'll go too, even though I don't want to. I feel
I'm leaving something precious behind.'

'Feel nothing like that.' Alexis's tone showed only
tartness. It held no regret, no nostalgia. He went on,
'These islands, this ocean, beautiful as they are, will
become so familiar to you that you'll come to recognise
them as your playground.'

Startled at these words, involuntarily her gaze swung to
him. But she was given no chance for further remarks.
Her hand was taken and she found she had no choice but
to run willy-nilly across the hot sand. Released, she found
her towel being spread for her beneath the close-growing
fringe of palm trees, and as she dropped down upon it,
Sarah asked, 'Put some stuff on my back and shoulders,
please, Clarissa,' so she smoothed on the sunscreen
lavishly, then combed her hair into the shape she wore it,
salt-encrusted and all. She watched the men as they
opened cartons and coolers, and soon glasses were being
passed around, and it was Alexis who came and knelt
down to offer her and Sophia tall containers of fruit juice
tinkling with ice.

He said, into the cloud of fair hair already drying in the
sun and breeze, 'Champagne later, fruit juice for now.'
He rose and took the beer Federico was offering to him,
while Frank was serving the older girls with tall frosted
glasses.

Clarissa was handed a plate by one servitor, cutlery by
another, her glass refilled by a third. And then she found
she had a luncheon companion. Alexis had smoothed the
sand and dropped down beside her.

She ate her meal—well, some of it—and knew it was
delicious even if she wasn't conscious of its taste. With
Alexis beside her, and so publicly, she had other things
than food to think about.

It was a leisurely meal. No one was in a hurry; everyone was happy, the food a delight, and the drinks icy, while above them palm fronds whispered and swayed.

As Clarissa reached for a salt-shaker Alexis' tanned shoulder was suddenly touching hers, and the tips of his fingers, on their way back, were travelling idly along her arm. The sun was hot, the atmosphere around them tropical—but she shivered. She withdrew from the vicinity of his body and thought, Damn you, Alexis. I just don't know how to take you.

Because actually, on this entire trip he had behaved so out of character. And even if she had vowed to be just a tourist and enjoy this weekend, this magical weekend, she had only expected him to be a pleasant host. Certainly not to behave as her actual escort.

And later, as she stood in the bow watching the launch inch into the jetty, she thought, so this is Dunk Island. The sun was low on the horizon behind them, and in front, floating on a blue ocean, was all that the words 'tropical island' conjured up. She turned for a moment to gaze back towards the mainland, then swung forward again as a tiny bump came. They had arrived!

Federico had jumped overboard and now the small gangway was being lowered. Beside it Alexis was speaking with Lesley, who stood with a proprietorial hand upon his arm.

Did she imagine she could get every male within clutching distance? thought Clarissa viciously, as she took her turn to step from the boat on to the hard planking.

A man was walking along it to meet them; middle-aged, pleasant, he was greeting first Federico and then Alexis. He began piloting them towards a minibus. Lesley was still close to Alexis, still also clinging to his arm, and was talking excitedly to the newcomer.

Then they were all inside the vehicle, and without knowing how it had come about, Clarissa found herself in a windowseat with Alexis seating himself beside her. From under downcast lashes she glanced swiftly up towards him. He was leaning across to speak to Eddie. She had noticed no manoeuvring, but there he was, beside her and not beside Lesley. Was this an example of that experience he had gathered over the years? she wondered, remembering.

And then all wondering had gone with the wind. He had turned to settle back in his seat and she felt the nearness of him so close. She turned—but it was to look out of her window.

Checked into charming motel rooms, Clarissa found she was paired off with Sophia after a soft voice had murmured into her ear, 'I've put you with Sophia, Clarissa. OK?'

And it was Sophia who was asking her now, 'Would you like the bathroom first, Clarissa? I'm always in trouble at home for taking too long, and as I want to wash my hair . . .' She gazed across at Clarissa, who found herself liking this girl. But she wondered what Sophia would think if she ever heard of that adventure in the cane fields with Federico. Still, to paraphrase Alexis, that was all water under the bridge.

Showered, shampooed, blow-dried, they were both waiting as they had been ordered to be by six-thirty, when Sophia said laughingly, 'You look beautiful, Clarissa, and Federico's mother would think so too. You look as if you'd just stepped from out of long-ago Greek history, while I, who am of Greek descent, look only like a modern young Australian.'

'Oh!' was all Clarissa could think to say, and she was relieved when a knock came on their door. Here we go, she thought, and straightened, tightening her expression as she went to meet Alexis. She found she had no need to do so. Outside stood Eddie with Alice and Sarah.

'Hi,' he greeted her. 'I've come to collect my harem,' then, giving a more encompassing look, he added, 'If I didn't have standing beside me who I have, I'd give a wolf whistle!' His hand reached out to take Alice's, who only smiled and nodded.

She said, 'Don't mind me, they deserve one.'

'You all deserve one,' said her fiancé. 'Come along and we'll see what next door has in store for us.' He knocked on it.

It was opened by Lesley, who said, 'Oh, Alexis . . .' then stopped, her glance going over the waiting group.

Interrupting before she could speak further, Eddie said, 'I've been sent to collect you all. Alexis is getting the drinks ready in the cabin.'

Clarissa could see Sarah looking at her, but kept her expression blank. Lesley looked perfect and charming as she always did. But she was wearing the white dress she had worn to Alexis' barbecue. Sarah, thank goodness, had gone shopping.

Clarissa and Sophia fell in behind the others as they walked along a green tunnel which hemmed them in, but also in its hedge tall coconut palms rose to a sky which was no longer turquoise but hazing to a pale duck-egg blue.

They came out before a cabin facing the ocean, low-set, merging into its setting, and on the veranda was the male contingent of their party clad in white tuxedos and dark trousers.

Alexis came to the top step to meet them, giving his attention to each one in turn. Federico slipped his arm through Sophia's, and then Alexis was looking her over. He said softly, his tone like the one he had used under the awning on the launch smooth, silken, 'Has anyone ever told you you're beautiful, Clarissa?'

She glanced quickly at him, then away, hoping her make-up hid the carnation red which had flooded her cheeks. But Alexis had turned and was speaking in his ordinary voice to the assembled guests. 'I've just been telling Clarissa to keep away from any spilling wineglasses. Because, before heaven, if *this* dress gets ruined, I'll go out there and drown myself!'

They were all laughing, thank goodness, noticed Clarissa, angry that he had brought that incident up. However, his words had also caused Lesley to look her over.

But their host was offering drinks, so she went to stand by the cabin railings to gaze outwards. She turned when Alexis came to her, holding out a long frosted glass.

'Everyone has to drink champagne tonight. Even Ray, who always opts for beer,' he said.

'Oh, not tonight!' called Ray, overhearing this remark. 'I intend to be the perfect guest and eat and drink all that's put before me.'

So, leaning against the rail, Clarissa sipped from her glass. Frank came over to stand beside her and the conversation became general.

They drank; they ate from the little dishes spread about; they teased Frank about his boat. Glasses were refilled, and it was seven-thirty when Alexis said, 'Dinnertime, I think.'

So again they walked through what was now only a dimly seen track, with soft romantic illumination to show them the way.

However, emerging, they found themselves in a blaze

of light. Met at their dining-room entrance, which was not the main one, they were seated at a round table. Lesley certainly had Alexis beside her, but then so did Clarissa.

No ordering was necessary. Seafood cocktails were being distributed, wineglasses were filled, and amid the laughter and conversation Clarissa remained silent, giving her attention to the meal before her. She found—which was not always the case when Alexis was around—that she could eat it easily.

Dishes removed, others taking their place, she saw she had a lobster with its big red tail facing her. A handsome tanned head leaned sideways; a low voice said, 'You told me once, I think, that you enjoyed seafood, Clarissa.'

Startled, she looked upwards and sideways, but only a sharp-cut profile was showing. Alexis had turned to speak smilingly to Lesley.

Thankfully, because there were no undercurrents in that direction, Clarissa gave her attention to Phil. He told her, 'Start on your lobster, Clarissa. It's delicious. Don't you agree, love?' The last few words were addressed to Sarah, who now leaned across him and looked laughingly into Clarissa's eyes. Both of them had recognised the proprietorial air with which Phil had spoken the word 'love'.

Clarissa got on with her meal. She didn't drink the different wine being now poured into her glass; she didn't like it as she had done the champagne. But she did enjoy the coffee afterwards, because it wasn't like any other coffee she had tasted.

Music had begun, and Alexis suggested they dance while they finished their wine, their coffee, their biscuits. And with Frank asking Lesley, he rose from his chair and held out a hand to her, saying, 'We'll have to see how we dance together, Clarissa. That too is another thing that we haven't yet done.'

Startled for the second time on this night of so many unexpected occurrences, not because of being asked to dance, but because of the words he had used, Clarissa placed her hand in his and went on to the tiny dance floor.

She danced in his arms, body close to body, feeling his length against her as she had on other occasions. The music was soft and lilting, the small floor polished and easy to glide over. Hadn't she said at one part of this day that this was happiness? She found now that that hadn't been entirely true. It was tonight, here at this moment, that that word described the whole atmosphere. Automatically she fitted her form closer into the confines of his, her arm around his neck going tighter.

She found herself swung round in a swift pirouette. She heard a curt voice saying as he set her apart, 'Stop it, Clarissa! A man can only take so much!'

Her step faltered; but his arm, iron-hard around her waist, went tight as she swayed, and she was gazing up into grey eyes, glinting with an expression she couldn't understand. She began to say, 'I'm sorry . . .' but that look changed suddenly and he was once again only the pleasant, smiling host that he had been on this entire outing.

He took hold of her hand, and swinging it between them, said, 'I think we've had enough dancing for tonight. There'll be other times!'

Federico and Sophia came to join them, and Clarissa found the talk drifting to wedding preparations, families and ceremonies. Among it all she discovered that Alexis was to be best man.

So, she thought—and wondered why he hadn't gone to

Federico for his explanations about that traumatic night. Abruptly he had turned as if catching her attention on him, and unexpectedly smiled caressingly at her. Her heart was suddenly not in its proper place.

'Were you wondering why I didn't go to Fred with my questions?' he asked, and laughed softly on seeing her expression change. 'I can always read what you're thinking, Clarissa. And I did go to him, only to find he'd left Ingham. That fact, I can tell you, was certainly not conducive to my peace of mind!'

A flurry of movement and talk was abruptly surrounding them. The dancers were back, and Alexis was suggesting a stroll down to the beach to see the moonlight on the water, and then bed. They had a full day's sailing before them in the morning, he was adding.

Everyone was agreeable to this suggestion, and again without discerning how it had been managed, Clarissa saw that Lesley was being partnered by Frank, while Alexis stayed behind to have a few words with the *maître d'*. As she made to follow the others, a hand reached out to prevent her.

Then she was strolling beside Alexis back along the tunnel of green through which moonlight now came in patches. Because of course, she thought sardonically, as it was Alexis' affair, there naturally would be moonlight!

Her hand was taken, fingers becoming interlaced with her own. Sounds echoed back towards them—from their own party and other guests on the island. But between themselves there was only silence. Once Federico turned to call something over his shoulder—in Spanish!

Alexis only laughed.

In a dream-haze Clarissa strolled, fingers still entwined with other fingers, until suddenly she was startled out of

her reverie. A beaten mirror of gleaming, glinting silver
was unexpectedly outspread before them.

But her companion had drawn back from that white
beach and scintillating water, to sweep her off the path
and into a dense clump of trees. He was setting her back
against the trunk of a large palm, and with both his hands
on either side of it her body was imprisoned between
them.

'This is stupid,' said Alexis' so different voice from
only inches away. 'I know . . . I do know what I've
decided—deliberately and in the cold light of day, but
as I told you once before tonight, a man can only take
so much . . . And I want you. Oh, how I want
you!'

And then the arms which had been imprisoning her
were doing so again, but in a different kind of way, one
along her shoulders, the other, spreadeagling low on her
back, bringing her into him completely.

She gasped. Tonight she wasn't seventeen on a
darkening river bank, or even in a bedroom with a man
who was exhibiting only violent anger and a brutal
demand. These caresses, these kisses being rained upon
her now were as if a need kept too long in check was
now being allowed to fulfil any clamouring purpose it
desired.

With their lower bodies locked together, Alexis was
bending her head backwards so that her hair lay loose
across his arm in a cascading fall of silver, while his lips
went on their plundering way along the exposed column
of her throat. And went further as fingers eased aside the
fragile material of her lovely Greek dress. Clarissa's eyes
closed.

Those searching, scorching caresses, on bare silken
skin, were bringing passion, desire, to both forms
entangled together beneath the tall whispering palms.

And all Clarissa wanted as she locked unyielding arms about his neck, moulded her body even yet closer to his, was for Alexis never to let her go . . . Only to continue with this lovemaking that was sliding her into a dimension she had never dreamed existed.

As if he had felt that need, that seeking, clamouring desire of a body being offered so freely to him, Alexis' hold tightened unbearably. So they stood, curves and hollows and muscles, fused completely, while the magic of this place, the vivid moonlight beyond them, the ebony shadows in which they were standing, spun. Spun, in a catherine wheel of brilliance . . . and all Clarissa could manage was to murmur, 'Alexis, Alexis,' as he swung her up to lower her upon the leaf-strewn sand.

But that action wasn't completed. She was suddenly set upright against the rough trunk of the tree behind her.

'!!!!!' The expletive came to her from where he stood, turned away a little, and it wasn't in Spanish, but in unadorned Australian. Then he said in completely unfamiliar tones, 'Well, there you are, Clarissa,' and derision against himself had crept into his voice. 'That little exhibition just now shows one of the reasons I'm so careful of starting anything with you. The other reason we'll go into when we get home.'

'Home,' Clarissa repeated hazily, with her body still not released from that searing, torrid lovemaking she had just experienced.

'Yes, tomorrow!' Alexis' tone was back to normal now. And as a shout echoed across the beach towards them, he took her arm and swung her round to face the footpath. 'How's your acting ability?' he asked. And the tone his voice carried swept away any vagueness and brought her abruptly back to this present moment, and to where they were. It had carried amusement—amusement! After experiencing those kisses, those . . . And Clarissa thought, as she had done so many times, I think I hate you, Alexis Markham.

Then they were stepping on to the beach. And of course it was Lesley who had called. She said now, 'We thought you must have got lost.'

'On this small island?' Alexis's eyebrows went high. 'Oh, no. I was speaking to the *maitre d'* about our lunch tomorrow. You'd better take off those shoes, Clarissa, if you're going to walk on the sand. Here, take my arm.'

The last sentence had been tacked on to his other speech, and, her glance flying to her feet, she saw that the other girls who were by now clustered about them had taken off their high-heeled shoes. So perforce she put first one hand and then the other on that white-clad arm held out to her, and slipped off her sandals.

Later, thinking about it, she knew they had all walked arm in arm along sand that the bright moonlight was turning to silver. She heard Federico singing in a voice so good that had them all joining in. She was not beside Alexis!

CHAPTER FOURTEEN

WHEN NEXT she surfaced to actually face the world, it was morning—a bright, sunlit morning. Sophia was coming from the bathroom. 'Oh, good morning, Clarissa,' she said. 'We have to pack and leave our cases ready before going to breakfast. OK?'

'It's certainly OK. I'll be ten minutes.' Clarissa smiled at the other girl, then slid out of bed and into the bathroom. As she gazed into the mirror, it was she this time who smiled derisively.

She shivered, thinking of last night, remembering. Alexis had said home . . . tomorrow . . . Well, today was tomorrow! So she would have to see what this tomorrow brought. And he had been so marvellous yesterday. What he had been last night—she didn't want to think about this morning. She stepped into the shower.

Then, clad in the new lemon shorts with the same coloured blouse and brief socks, she bent down to tie the laces of her white canvas sneakers. Hair brushed, having applied a heavier foundation than she normally did to filter this northern sun's heat, she carefully smoothed on lipstick and went into the bedroom. Sophia turned from looking out of the window and said, 'It's just as well I'm wearing white! Lemon suits you, Clarissa.'

Clarissa replied blithely, vowing to begin the day as she meant to go on, 'Yes, yellow is my colour, but you should worry! Look how your skin gleams against the white.'

It was with complacency that Sophia answered, 'Yes, I know. So I try to wear it as much as I can. We'll go and complement one another. Here, is that your case finished? Shove it over here with mine.'

Clarissa ate breakfast—not sitting beside Alexis. She went on the scenic walk to the top of the hill. But there, suddenly, the beauty of it and the prospect outspread before her brought her back to life. This island really was a paradise. Alexis looked across and smiled at her, pleasantly, warmly. But it was only with gravity that she returned that look.

Then it seemed that the exodus came so swiftly, that in a short time she was standing at the front of the boat as it edged away from the jetty. She gazed back, thinking that no matter if she went from this far northern country, or stayed, this place before her would always be remembered as a paradise island.

Ray came to stand beside her. He said, 'Do you know that I came up here only to do my stint in the outback, but look about you! I think I might have to be doing some rethinking.'

'But, Ray,' Clarissa was laughing, 'this isn't the outback. The outback is much farther west.'

'Well, when I had to take this post, I thought it was; but heigh-ho! Let's see what this day has in store for us.'

It had in store sailing through blue, sunlit waters; it didn't have swimming. But it had a gourmet lunch, eaten on deck, which the tourist complex had put up for them. They enjoyed it anchored off a small uninhabited island.

And then almost without realising it they had entered the river leading towards home and were easing into the old wooden jetty. Then with seemingly no time wasted they were on their way. Alexis dropped Phil off at the barracks, then at the girls' house he said, 'I want to borrow you for an hour or so, Clarissa. Sophia wants to

consult you about wedding presents. Would you
mind?'

Here we go again! Clarissa thought. But what could she
say? And what a thing for Alexis to suggest! But Sarah
and Alice, descending from the Jaguar, were only saying,
'Thank you for such a wonderful weekend, Alexis. See
you, Clarissa.'

The car drove off, and again as had so often happened
there was only silence between them. But Clarissa didn't
need to ask where they were going. The familiar road to
her companion's farm was coming up to meet them, and
then sliding past.

Alexis slid out, opened her door, and with light fingers
on her elbow guided her through the back door and into
the kitchen. He said, 'Now, you sit on that side and I'll sit
on this one. We have things to discuss and decisions to be
made.'

In the event, he still reached out and took hold of her
wrist as it lay on the table between them, and with his
thumb stroked the pale inside back and forth. Clarissa
closed her eyes. She said, 'Don't!'

Then, making herself look at him, she saw him smile,
and her heart lurched—she felt it.

Alexis said, 'And that's a word which I want wiping
from your vocabulary. Because I'll be doing that . . . and
other things where I don't want to hear you saying,
"Don't!"'

'But now to serious matters. You know, Clarissa, we
didn't get off to the normal ordinary start, did we? Oh,
the way I behaved . . . kissing a schoolgirl, and in the
heavy way I did . . . It was shameful!

'No,' interrupting, Clarissa shook her head, 'if I'd
shown the least objection, or appeared frightened, it
wouldn't have developed as it did. But I was already in
love with you. It happened while I was flying on a

windsurfer, schoolgirl or not.'

It was Alexis' turn to shake his head, saying, 'I did nearly ride past, you know. But you *were* in a dangerous place. Crocodiles have been known to come out and sun themselves on that bank . . .' He stopped speaking and his thumb went back and forth more sharply.

'You knew Delys,' he went on. 'You saw how beautiful she was?'

'Oh yes, indeed,' interrupted Clarissa. 'Absolutely, devastatingly beautiful!'

'Well, I met her, saw her, fell in love, or so I thought, all within ten days—but then at twenty-four, with not a lot of experience, one is inclined to fall for absolutely stunning girls. But at least I had the sense to make one stipulation when they wanted the marriage to take place in Sydney before we came home. And that was that Delys came up to see the far north before the situation became irrevocable. God, or Fate, or Karma, must have been watching out for me.'

Alexis rose from his chair and came to sit beside her on the table's edge. His hand resting on his thigh still held and stroked her wrist, however. He said, 'Well, I was driving to town to a meeting, and found I'd forgotten some papers and had to go back for them. There was no mistaking the scene between the two I found there! He was her cousin and had followed her. They'd been in love for always, said Delys. But she'd been brought up to marry a rich man. And of course I fitted that bill.' Alexis laughed, and it wasn't a pleasant sound.

And the tone his voice carried when he resumed speaking wasn't pleasant either. It held a harsh ruthlessness. 'If I'd needed anything to tell me, show me, the difference in the way I felt about you and Delys, it was in the manner I dealt with a situation I felt was similiar to you both. Where Delys came towards me with a hand entreatingly outstretched, I couldn't bear to be touched by her. I just wanted her gone. I arranged it! And when they'd left, both of them, I saddled Thunder and tried to ride off some of the furious aversion I felt by galloping wild.

'However, with you, Clarissa. Oh, with you, when I thought you were with Fred on that comedy of errors night, it was an entirely different matter. I had every intention of making you pay. There was no idea at all of my not wanting to be touched by you. I was going to make love to you—all night long if I felt so inclined.

'Then, of course, I found out what had actually happened. And it was I who wanted to come to you with an entreating hand outstretched. I also saw how it would be received. Your expression carried only deep, active dislike. So . . .' His thumb had finally stopped stroking her wrist, but he had raised it and his lips were taking over the occupation it had been engaged upon.

'So,' he repeated, when once more he had deposited her wrist on his thigh, 'I had to begin all over again. But you must admit,' another tone had crept into the disclaiming voice, 'that I certainly put on a good show this weekend.

'Clarissa, I want you! This is today's world and I would be within my rights to pick you up and carry you to my bedroom. And don't think I haven't thought of it. But it wouldn't be that first fine careless rapture which our lovemaking should be. Because with you I have a mental blockage. So will you marry me right away?'

Her wrist was nearly released as she jerked sharply upright. She said, 'What a thing to say, and just out of the blue like that! Also, what do you mean by right away? I sounds so . . . so . . .'

Alexis was laughing at her words, her tone. He told her, 'I meant exactly that! Right away! You have a holiday break in only three weeks, don't you? We can be married then.'

'Yes, I do have a holiday break, in September. But you're mad, Alexis! No one can arrange a wedding in three weeks.'

'I'm not mad! Of course anyone can arrange a marriage in three weeks. I can! And if it comes to that, I could most likely arrange it in three days. Now . . .' he paused for a moment and looked at her, 'there's a thought! A time of only three days away would suit me very well.'

Horrified, eyes wide open, Clarissa gazed back at him. 'You're not just mad, Alexis, you're crazy,' she said breathlessly.

'No, I'm not. But look, I'll be generous. I'll give you a choice. You can either marry me in September, or you can live here as my mistress, lover, or whatever . . . starting from tonight, if that's what you choose.'

She stood immobile, and just looked at him. She saw in his handsome bronzed face harsh indented lines she had never noticed before, the ruthlessness that his whole demeanour showed. She said suddenly, 'All right!'

For a moment he was silent, then he asked, 'You did say all right. And it did mean what I think it means.'

Yes, I did say all right. What other choice did I have?'

'Oh, come now, Clarissa,' he was speaking gently, but a lopsided grin stretched his lips. 'I did give you a choice. Surely you remember that?'

'Yes, I do remember. And you would have looked silly if I'd decided on the other one.'

'Oh, but knowing you, I knew I was safe. Now I expect we'd better let your mother know.'

'Oh, good heavens! What shall I say?'

'*You* needn't say anything. I'll ring her after I've taken you home. I want only my suggestions put across, not yours.

'But I'll allow you the choice of your wedding day. It can be on the Saturday through to Wednesday. That will give us ten days for a honeymoon before we have to get back.'

'Would there be any hurry, though?' Clarissa knew she was only talking for talking's sake. She felt that if she were to take in the underneath meaning of all this discussion, it would be like last night. The entire scene would disintegrate into a blazing catherine wheel, and this time it would engulf her.

'But of course all your cane wouldn't have been cut yet,' she was continuing, to only have her words waved nonchalantly aside.

'No, it hasn't,' he agreed. 'However, that doesn't matter. It's that you have to be back at school when it reopens.'

If Clarissa had looked horrified before, she looked aghast now. 'You don't really think I'll go back and teach—after marrying you in a term break and going away on a honeymoon, do you? You must be mad, Alexis!'

'And you, my love, should remember that I'm the P and C President. I like living here and it's my district. They can get a new teacher next year, but having to find one for the last ten weeks wouldn't be appreciated.'

'But, Alexis——' Her words were cut off. Alexis had finally released her wrist and had slid from his perch on the table. He pulled her upright as well, and stood her away. He said, his glance running over her, 'Just look at you in those short shorts that . . .'

'They're not short shorts; they're the regulation length. I don't wear those minuscule ones, thank you very much,' she interrupted.

Alexis only laughed. 'Well, short or not, a bloke isn't in his right mind to have a girl like you, dressed like that, with only a big empty house around him—and especially realising as I do the way your just being here affects me.'

He gazed down into her eyes, and suddenly all talk of weddings, of anything extraneous, fell away, and they were looking at one another with only one thought, one absolute knowledge, in both their glances. Alexis' head came down and, as her body was brought into him, his lips on her cheek followed her jawline down along the thrown-back throat, to come to rest where the buttons of the lemon blouse were no longer fastened.

Clarissa closed her eyes, feeling the jumping nerves that coiled and twisted within her entire being. This caress, so different, was a sexual attack upon her whole metabolism. She couldn't move, she could only stand motionless, enclosed, waiting . . .

After what could have been an eternity, or a shuddering heartbeat, Alexis had released her and turned sideways. She saw his hand upon the edge of the table, its tan turning to grey as his grip tightened.

Frightened, she moved round to face him, saying, 'Alexis, it doesn't matter! Whatever you want, I'll do. Alexis . . .'

He turned then, and even if it was a little strained, it was still a smile he gave to her. 'Yes, I know,' he answered. 'But for tonight I think it's time I took you home.' He walked to the door, and opening it, stood aside.

He stood aside also after opening the door of the Jaguar. And once again the ride was accomplished in silence. Gazing carefully across at his face, Clarissa saw that it showed only an uncompromising hardness.

However, on pulling to a stop before their house, he said, 'Look, Clarissa, just relax and enjoy these last few weeks. I will see to and arrange everything, I promise you.'

'Yes, Alexis, I expect you can and will. However, when this news gets out, no one will dare say anything to you, or even look remotely sideways at you. But *I'm* not Alexis Markham, wealthy, handsome, and the most eligible man in the whole district.'

'Good heavens, Clarissa! Fair go! But if I'm the kind of man you've just described—rather inaccurately, I suggest—*you* are the girl I want to marry, so that's all you have to think about, and also all you have to give as an answer. And I tell you again, everything will turn out just as you'd want it to. Now, can you go and break the news to your two friends up there?'

'Oh yes, I expect I can do that! Alexis . . . I know how I feel about you, but do you . . .?'

Suddenly the tension and strain which had been all about them in the confined space of the front seat disintegrated. Alexis was bending over, laughing. And, wildly angry at this reaction to her words, Clarissa went to unfasten her seat-belt and go.

A hand reached out to prevent her. 'Look, Clarissa,' Alexis's voice was still unsteady, 'don't ever worry about my feelings for you. Just know that more than anything I want you, need to have you. Now, go up there and do the one chore you have to do concerning your own wedding.'

He leant across to finish unfastening her seat-belt, and said, 'I'm not coming up with you. I have to go home and get myself back to the real world, and I don't need you with me to do that. So off you go!'

Clarissa went, and only saw a hand wave from the car window as she began to walk up the steps. Her fingers on the veranda door, she drew in a deep breath and walked inside. Sarah was lying on the sofa; Alice at the dining-room table drinking from a cup smiled across the room at her, saying, 'Sarah didn't want anything. I'm having a cup of coffee, but I don't expect you'd like one.'

'No, I'll go and make tea,' answered Clarissa, and moved into the kitchen. Anything, she thought wryly, to put off what she had to say.

'I'll have tea if you're making it, Clarissa,' called out Sarah. 'And a couple of those savoury biscuits with cheese.'

Clarissa finished making the snack and carried Sarah's in to her, then went to sit beside Alice. After sipping the hot beverage for a few seconds, she began, 'I have something to tell you,' then exclaimed baldly, 'Alexis asked me to marry him tonight and I said yes.'

For a few seconds only silence answered her, then Sarah choked on her tea and pushing the cup jerkily out of her way, swung abruptly round to face the other two.

'*What* . . .? What did you say?' she then got out breathlessly.

'You heard what I said.'

'But I'm sure I didn't hear it right! Alexis . . .!' The second syllable of the man's name echoed loudly throughout the room.

'Well, *I* knew you were interested in someone after our little talk that other morning, but I didn't dream of it being Alexis. However, I should have,' chimed in Alice.

'I was here last year, and so were you, Sarah. But we were never invited to barbecues at that fabulous house, or to weekend sailing outings by Alexis, now were we?'

'No, I don't suppose we were. But *Alexis!*' And again when she spoke his name, Sarah's voice went high in disbelief. Then abruptly she collapsed into giggles, and as the other two girls looked at her impatiently she told them, 'I was only thinking that if Phil and I also got engaged, all three of us could be getting married as soon as school breaks up at the end of the year. Now wouldn't that be something? A triple wedding!'

'Except,' Clarissa made herself say, 'that we won't be getting married in December! Our ceremony is to be at the beginning of September term holidays.'

'Oh!' The irrepressible Sarah spoke only the one word before shooting a glance across at Alice.

'And whatever you're thinking, it's wrong.' Acid etched Clarissa's words. Then glancing at both girls, she abruptly grinned and added, 'Would you believe me if I told you that Alexis said he can't wait until December to marry me? Because that's what he *did* say.'

Sarah's eyes flew open wide and she said eagerly, 'Tell us! Just tell us all about it. Because you know, Clarissa, I can't imagine how it happened. I wouldn't have suspected that you'd seen Alexis more than a few times.' She paused for a moment before adding carefully, 'You said he wanted to marry you. I expect, seeing who it is that we're discussing, it's silly asking if you want to marry him?'

'Oh, yes,' wryness coloured Clarissa's answer, 'I expect it is, because I've been in love with him since

practically the first time we met.' And she had been but
these two watching her didn't know how long ago that had
been, and she had no intention of telling them.

'Look,' she said, rising from her chair, 'I'm going to
bed. Alexis has told me that he will arrange everything, so
that's what I'm going to allow him to do. I do, however,
wish him joy of his interview with our boss, because I
hope not to be there. He can be the recipient of any
exchanges or looks like that one Sarah gave just a few
minutes ago. Goodnight, I'm leaving.'

She went.

CHAPTER FIFTEEN

THE WHEELS of the big Jaguar were sending the miles behind them, more quickly than Clarissa had noticed Alexis ever driving before. And these were country roads; the main highway up towards Cairns, certainly, but it was not a broad four-laned highway. It twisted and turned as country roads were inclined to do.

From under downcast lashes, surreptitiously, she sent a sideways glance in her companion's direction, then, remembering his strictures on that mannerism of hers, she opened her eyes wide. However, she didn't continue looking at him. She turned and gazed out of the window.

But with the fingers of one hand she felt the third finger of the other one. Felt the engraved wedding band, the sapphire and diamond engagement ring. Both had been given to her this morning, the plain golden one in a church when the minister had told Alexis to do so, the gleaming blue and white one in the vestry afterwards.

'A little late,' came murmured in a soft voice from the man who was bestowing it, 'but you must admit things were a trifle hurried.' Clarissa could have hit him as she took note of that raised eyebrow, the pleasant, give-away-nothing of that social smile. For whose fault had it been, this hurried wedding?

But then she had actually looked at it, and then quickly up at Alexis—her husband, who had turned away to sign his name. Almost frightened, she was casting a second glance at the gleaming, glittering object, when someone had said, 'Now you, Mrs Markham.' She had signed, hearing her new name for the first time and ignoring it, because the beautiful ring had been taking all her attention.

And also later, if she hadn't known that Alexis was in love with her—or that he said he was, and he certainly acted like it when they were alone—anyone would have thought he was performing his part in the affair under duress. He certainly smiled at her when they came in contact with one another. But he didn't touch her, or put an arm around her, or even kiss her after the ceremony, which she had noticed happening at other weddings she had attended.

From the church they had driven to Alexis' home. And instead of the quiet gathering she had anticipated, she had walked into the midst of what seemed like hundreds of guests. Practically all the district, she thought, bemused. She had then thought differently, acid coating the reflection, that if anyone had had the thought that this wedding was a hole-and-corner affair, they were being shown otherwise. Because it was being presented with all the pomp and ceremony that the male part of it could contrive.

Champagne ran like coloured water, and as it was a luncheon reception waiters were there to encourage appetites with every kind of food Clarissa was aware of, and so many—again she thought astringently—of which she was not.

Sarah and Alice came up to admire her ring. Clarissa had kept it hidden turned around. A big blue Australian sapphire mounted high in a surround of diamonds, it was hardly a ring to be worn doing the housework, and she knew that actually she would have preferred one she could have worn constantly.

Her mother looked at it and smiled. 'Never mind,

Clarissa,' she had said, reading her daughter's expression. 'Just think of its giver and you'll love it,' and then she had patted Clarissa's shoulder as a burning rush of colour flooded the young girl's cheeks.

Yes, of course, if she thought of its bestower, she wouldn't have cared if it had been as big as the Koh-i-noor or as small as the tiniest diamond engagement ring, but now she only said, 'At least I can show off my wedding dress,' and indicated the lovely creation of floating chiffon dropping to mid-calf in a myriad fall of tiny pleats. 'And you, Mother, can take the credit for it.' It had been procured from one of her mother's contacts in Brisbane.

Sophia too, whom she had asked to be her bridesmaid, because after all, Federico was to be Alexis' best man, was dressed in an almost similar creation, but in the palest lavender. Looking at the dresses when they had arrived, Clarissa had remarked smilingly, 'Well, Sophia, you won't be in your favourite white on that day.'

'No, I won't! But don't forget my day is coming. I'll wear white then. We're both lucky, Clarissa, aren't we?' Sophia had added.

Yes, they were. Clarissa acknowledged it, but she also acknowledged that for her everything would not be all plain sailing. She knew that with Alexis in love with her as he seemed to be, she would still have to tread warily.

For now, she only wished he would talk, even if in only ordinary conversation. It could have been almost a stranger who had been waiting beside Federico at the altar steps. Then, as if they had been in silent communication, Alexis turned and said, 'Cardwell coming up now, we'll be there in a minute.' The large vehicle was slowing and its driver turned, stroking the back of his fingers down her cheek.

Reaching up, she placed her own upon them and gave to him the most radiant smile she could dredge up.

'!!!!' Again she heard that expletive as she had done once before, but Alexis was continuing, 'I knew what I was about in keeping away from you at that damned reception. If you'd smiled at me like that I wouldn't have been responsible for my actions. Now it doesn't matter if I act irresponsibly. We're here!'

They had driven through a small township and had stopped opposite what appeared to be the ocean on its very doorstep. And at a small landing lay a cabin-cruiser at anchor.

A voice called, 'Hi there, mate!'

Alexis was grinning as he stepped from the car. Walking round to open the passenger-side door, he replied over a shoulder, 'Mate yourself! Don't start telling me about the one that got away—or even more truthfully about the ones that didn't.' He helped Clarissa to alight, but his attention was clearly on the man waiting beside the boat.

He said as he pulled out their suitcases, 'Will you go with Bert, Clarissa, while I put the Jaguar away?'

Feeling abandoned, she watched him slide from behind the wheel of the car. This man was surely not dressed as a man going on his honeymoon would dress, in much washed brown cords, in a short-sleeved brown knitted shirt. But he had told her, 'Don't dress up, Clarissa. Wear something old, just as ordinary holidaymakers would wear.'

So she hadn't dressed up, she decided as she gazed down at the blue linen shift which swung about her. With a large pocket on either side and zipped from hem to throat, it just gave the appearance of being a favourite old-time dress.

She followed Bert and a youth who had picked up the cases, and on the cruiser went to stand in the cockpit. She turned from the mainland to gaze seawards. Yes, there it was; a smudge of green rising from the gleaming ocean of blue that surrounded it—her paradise island.

Then two things occurred at once. The engine of the boat purred into sound and Alexis had come to stand beside her. Bert said, 'Would you like to come in here, miss, and sit down?'

Alexis reached out long brown fingers and drew her to where he was lounging on the wall behind him. The casual arm he then placed about her shoulders showed no sign of being a romantic practice; it held no hint of passion or desire. And, cocooned in that clasp, she heard him say, 'This is my wife, Clarissa, Bert.'

'Oh, good on you, mate. It's about time too. Hi there, Clarissa,' said Bert. And that was all the conversation in which she was included. But then *she* didn't go fishing!

However, she remained within the embrace of that casual clasp; a clasp which said they had been married forever. And she realised that this impression given was the reason that worn clothes and old luggage had been stipulated. Alexis knew, and was known to, all these people; and honeymooners created an attention he could do without.

She only half listened to the talk about big fish—these waters were marlin habitats—but she felt that arm around her; an arm, an embrace, which had never before been so publicly in evidence. And, unable to help herself, she moved closer into it as she gazed ahead to see this island of hers drifting so close.

She stepped out on to the same jetty—if from a different boat. And they were being met by the same man driving the same minibus. But they were not taken to the same motel rooms.

The little vehicle made its slow journey along a track winding between close-growing rain-forest. It came to a stop before a cabin like the one that they had had drinks in that memorable weekend.

The cases set down on the veranda, they had been waved to and were suddenly alone. Alexis was picking up the bags and telling her with only a half-smile, 'Well, here we are, Clarissa, so let's go and find out what the gods have in store for us.'

She glanced quickly up at him. Those words sounded strange, sombre, but she followed him through the open door into a living-room. Not at all a sophisticated set-up liked the one she and Sophia had shared, went the thought through her mind. This dwelling was fashioned to fit into its setting, with rush mats on the floor and cane furniture scattered around.

She wasn't given a lot of time to stand and stare. Alexis had pushed open a door leading out of it, and had walked across a bedroom to put the cases on the luggage rack by a window made of glass.

She turned to smile at her companion, forgetting for the moment who he was—and what this day was. They could have been standing in the open out-of-doors, among a forest of shrubs and palms, cunningly fashioned and gardened to present such an atmosphere.

Alexis was standing away from her against the far wall. He said, 'I expect we should get some unpacking done. It's around five now and we could go for a walk before dinner. OK?'

'Yes, of course OK.' Unclipping the catches of her case, Clarissa took out dresses and began to smooth them

on hangers. Then with her hands full of toilet
bottles she swung round to the dressing table and
unexpectedly met his gaze. He hadn't begun at all on his
unpacking.

Clarissa came to a full stop, feeling the atmosphere
which had so suddenly changed about them. Alexis said,
'Have I told you before how beautiful you are,
Clarissa?'

With the bottles still clasped in her hands, unable to
move to set them down, she began to speak. She found
she couldn't, so started again.

'Yes, you have—once. Here on this island. But I
assumed it was only a host being pleasant to his guest. I
took no notice, because with all your faults, Alexis, I've
never included telling lies among them.'

Only a sound which certainly couldn't be described as a
laugh erupted from him. Then he spoke. 'I'm afraid it
wouldn't have been telling lies today. I turned to look at
you walking up the aisle, and suddenly you were a
different person . . .'

'Oh, that!' interrupted Clarissa, suddenly finding that
she could act normally again and dispose of the bottles.
'That wasn't me. That was my mother.'

But Alexis' voice when he replied didn't carry
normality at all. It came coloured with perplexity. 'Your
mother?' he was asking, puzzlement uppermost.

'Oh, yes. I've never used a lot of make-up. I've
never had the money, for one thing, and I was too busy
studying for my degree for another. However, my
mother . . . In her job she had to look sophisticated,
elegant. And make-up was a part of that. She really is
good at it, you know.

'So when I have anything special on, today for
instance, she uses her expertise on me. You wouldn't
believe how many different lines, how many different

colours and brush strokes went into preparing me for my
wedding . . .' Abruptly, Clarissa broke off, her last words
conjuring up all that was the meaning of this day; the
meaning of that ceremony.

But by then Alexis had taken only two steps, two long
steps, and his arms were about her. He didn't kiss her.
But in his embrace, so close to him, she could feel the
tremor, the tiny rippling shudder that was passing
through him.

Then, muffled in her hair, she heard him say, 'I know
all the things I should do, and all the things I
shouldn't do, but will you bear with me, my love?' And
then his head came down and his lips were upon
hers.

On tiptoe she went to meet him—on bare tiptoes,
having kicked off her sandals while unpacking—but then
found herself stood away. He had done two things
then—reached out and further flung away a quilt which
was already turned down for the night, and then, gazing
into her eyes, taken hold of the little anchor at the top of
her zip and pulled. He had gone on pulling.

The dress parted and his fingers had smoothed the
sleeves from her shoulders. All she had to do was step
from it. She did!

His lips were moving slowly, sensuously along her
throat, and his hand on her back unclipped the one hook
there. Kisses went plundering down to where a scrap of
nylon and lace had belonged but which was gone now. In
a tone she didn't recognise, he said, 'I want you so much,
Clarissa,' and picked her up and dumped her on the bed.

Outspread, fair, shining hair cascading over the white
pillows, she put up her arms and Alexis came to her. The
second scrap of nylon and lace was brushed aside, and
then came the kisses she had gone so happily to meet on

this same island. But they had now taken on a deeper intensity, turning into caresses that carried scorching heat, searing desire.

She heard his voice penetrating that haze of passion which enclosed them both, as with husky, uninhibited murmurs he was entreating her, 'Forget everything; don't even think; just come with me, my love.'

So she went, finding new steps to conquer along the way, as his lips, his hands, his very breath brought her new heights to be scaled. Until suddenly there was nothing about them except the flaming, crimson passion that made her gasp although she did not know it. And then came those kisses, soul-searching, seeking, which brought her arching to him with memory gone, and nothing about her in the entire world but this man, this lover who was her other self.

When next she realised she was thinking, when reality and an outside existence had surfaced around her, she lay still, not wanting to talk, wanting only to remember. Alexis had gone from her and lay, a heavy arm flung completely across her. She turned her head carefully and could distinguish only a profile with unruly damp hair falling over eyes that were closed.

Just as carefully she turned her head back again, then spoke very quietly. 'Alexis . . .'

He didn't answer; his body didn't move, but as if his subconsciousness had become aware, his arm across her tightened. He was asleep!

Was that good or bad? she wondered, then turned to gaze out of the window. And even as she watched, darkness was taking over from the short twilight of this far northern country; the rain-forest growing shadowy and dim.

Again moving carefully, she reached behind for a

pillow and pulled it down. Slipping it between the deeply unconscious form and herself, she slid out, easing the heavy arm across it.

Catching up the short housecoat she had carelessly thrown over the suitcase lid, she turned and glanced at the sleeping figure on the bed. She thought suddenly that Alexis looked older; lines more deeply indented around the side of the mouth that she could see. She told herself that she was being silly. His image had been in her memory from long years ago, and that was probably what she remembered.

She moved softly into the bathroom. Then, showered and dried, she went back into the bedroom. Picking up a brush, she walked to the window and stroked it smoothly through her hair. It was fully dark now outside.

What made her realise she was being watched, she couldn't afterwards have said. There had been no movement. But she turned quickly, and in the faint starlight entering from outside she saw that Alexis, now leaning against the pillows behind him, was looking at her.

He said, and there echoed a sound of anger in the low voice, 'Wouldn't you know that with the way I've made a mess of our whole relationship, I'd do the same with tonight? To end up going to sleep!'

Clarissa walked the few steps to the bed and gazed down at him. She said, 'Do I have any say about tonight? Unlike you, Alexis, I had no experience to compare it with, but tonight brought me everything I could desire . . .'

She wasn't allowed to continue. A hand had reached out to bring her to him, and with lips against bare perfumed skin Alexis said, 'Don't think I won't make later on much more than everything you could desire.

That I promise you! For now, the only excuse I have for going fathoms down in that sleep is that it's been evading me almost completely of late.'

For a long moment only silence reigned in the room about the two motionless forms; then, in an entirely different tone, with his head still pressed against her, he said, 'Besides being beautiful, you smell wonderful too.'

'Oh, that.' Clarissa gazed at the dark head lying on her breast, and forcefully prevented her hand moving out to stroke it. She only repeated lightly, 'Oh, that's not me. That's my new perfume, and buying it was an extravagant act on my part. However . . .' she paused, then continued, 'I thought that seeing who I was to marry it wouldn't matter if I indulged myself in wickedly expensive French perfume, and that you wouldn't mind if I have to come to you for a hand-out.'

The dark head came up, and she was pulled completely down and enfolded to him. He said, laughing into her eyes, 'When you do do a thing, my love, you do it handsomely! Didn't I promise this morning that on thee I bestowed all my worldly goods? Take them all to buy perfume and then lead me to paradise.

'But for now, I expect that I too had better set about making myself as presentable as you are.'

Alexis had rolled over with that single fluid movement she had noticed of him when sliding behind the wheel of his car, and was off the bed. She saw the bathroom light flash on and then the door shut.

Reaching out a hand, she pressed down a switch of the bedside lamp, then, also rolling off the bed—but not with the grace of Alexis, she was sure—she went over to turn on the overhead light.

As she surveyed the disarray fo the whole room, a wry smile touched her lips. She bent to gather up her bra and pants and put them in a laundry bag; to take up the blue shift, zip it up and smooth it along a hanger. Alexis's cords folded over a chair, she then surveyed the bed.

The shower was running so, having time, she gathered up the shirt, twisted and crumpled from lying beneath its owner, and sent it too into the laundry bag. She then returned the bed to its former pristine appearance.

The shower had stopped running, so, swiftly donning clean underclothes and a yellow cotton dress, Clarissa gazed at her reflection. Yes, it looked fine. Not of course like the exclusive creation of a similar colour that Alexis had sent her; this frock had come off a chain-store rack. But as he seemed to like her in any shade of gold, she had bought it.

Now, a smoothing in of foundation, some brushes of highlight, a tinge of oil on her brows to keep them in line, and she was ready. Not looking as outstandingly glamorous as she had done earlier today—but ready.

Wishing to allow Alexis all the space and time he needed, she left, going through the living-room and out on to the veranda. There, her face raised to the heavens, she gazed up at the brilliantly shining stars, glittering diamonds spread out for inspection on a black velvet canopy. Yes, there it was, the Southern Cross.

She smiled. Always there, always looked for, it had provided her with a sense of security in her night outings and growing up days. But for now, drawing in a deep breath of the cool, ocean breeze, she brought her thoughts back to the present, glad of these few solitary minutes to be alone.

But it *was* only a few minutes that she was alone.

Her husband had come to join her, putting what was probably wallet and keys into his trouser pockets. He was dressed in only dark pants and a thin white roll-collared top.

Clarissa exclaimed without thinking, 'I didn't expect you so soon. You've only been a few minutes . . .' She abruptly stopped.

'But then,' said an amused voice, a normal voice, 'I haven't got to sit before a mirror, taking an hour or so to prepare my face for a night's entertainment.'

'I don't do that either!' the answer came indignantly, then went on in a different tone, 'But it appears you know all about what females do when dressing for an evening.' The last words were in a different tone, and they were tartly acid.

Only amusement coloured the laugh which answered her. Then, taking her arm, Alexis walked her down the steps. They strolled, slowly, companionably along the path, always with Alexis indicating the way, and once, as he was casually speaking, a blazing memory of what had occurred this evening overcame her without warning.

For a moment her breath caught, her step faltered. And then Alexis' arm was around her, his voice asking, 'Are you OK?'

'Yes, my foot just caught in a root.' The lie came easily, and she walked on with his fingers holding her arm. She hadn't meant that scene to flash before her vision. It had come out of the blue. It would take time . .

Thankfully she allowed her thoughts to be interrupted. They had emerged into a blaze of light. The familiar dining-room was before them.

And it was also the familiar *maître d'* who came to conduct them to their table. A table for two against a window—not the large round one about which they had all congregated when last here. The room too was a little different, fairly crowded with other guests.

Tonight they had to order, the food not being just set before them. Clarissa chose a sole Mornay with a side salad. Alexis ordered steak Diane and Clarissa watched fascinated as it was prepared at their table. She didn't think she would like it with all that taste of alcohol.

Alexis saw her expression and grinned. He told her, an eyebrow raised, '*I* didn't eat at that reception, so I think I'm entitled to indulge myself at dinner. Wasn't that the phrase you used about French perfume?'

She couldn't give him the answer he had given to her on that subject, so she just looked away and concentrated on eating her food. She drank half of the wine poured into her glass; she liked champagne better.

The meal over, they rose as others were doing on being informed that the entertainment was about to begin. With two other couples they sat on a settee, clapped the singers and laughed at the comic turns. Then came the music for dancing, modern and loud.

'Would you rather dance or go for a walk to the beach?' Alexis asked.

'For tonight, Alexis, I'd rather go to the beach. I only wore low-heeled flatties to walk to the restaurant. They're not suitable for dancing, I'm sorry to say,' she answered, wondering what he would want to do.

'I'm not sorry.' A pleased smile was directed at her. 'I'm glad you wore only walking shoes. We can dance another night. Off we go.'

Outside, again Clarissa trod the path which she had walked before with this man beside her, but they were in company tonight. Others had left the dancing and were drifting down to the beach or wending their way home. It could be an early call for a long day's fishing on the morrow.

Passing the thick clump of trees close to the water
Alexis pulled her to his side, saying, 'I don't need t
kidnap you behind that lot tonight, so we'll proceed lik
any ordinary couple and walk the beach on the wa
home.'

Clarissa kept silent. No, he didn't need to kidnap he
tonight, she thought. She only asked, however, 'Can w
go along the sand to our cabin? We didn't go to it tha
way.'

'No, we didn't. Because we drove . . .' Alexis ducke
as two flying figures almost careered into him
putting out a hand to steady the feminine half c
the duo. He continued speaking as if the sma
interruption hadn't happened, 'But along the beach thi
way it's only a hundred yards or so. Look, here we are a
the beginning of the track. Take my arm and empty you
shoes.'

Having no option, Clarissa put a hand on the har
forearm held out to her, stood on one foot, emptied
shoe, performed the same service with the other, whil
thinking, you know too much altogether about women
Alexis. But all she did was walk quietly along besid
him.

The cabin when they came to it was a blaze of light. C
course, the man beside her had been the last one out an
had left every light burning as he went. Clarissa shook he
head.

In the living-room, Alexis said, 'I'm going to have
drink. Would you care for anything, Clarissa?'

'No . . . no, thank you. I had drinks while I wa
listening to those singers.' She went past him into th
bedroom, where for a moment she stood motionless
Then, shrugging, she undressed and, taking out
nightdress, looked it over. It was cotton, but not a cotto

she had ever been familiar with. Almost sheer, it had a V-neckline lace and ribbon-edged—and it would show her every outline.

She donned it and, in the bathroom, cleaned off her make-up and brushed her teeth. Then taking a necessary deep breath she went back into the bedroom.

Clad in a short maroon towelling robe, Alexis was there standing before the window. He was holding a squat cut-glass tumbler. An eyebrow went up as he looked her over.

'You didn't carry my admonitions about old and ordinary clothes into sleeping gear, I see,' he told her. 'That looks very fetching.'

'And so it should! Like the French perfume, this handful of material was right outside my budget too. Still, for its purpose . . .' Astringency coloured the tone.

Alexis laughed, and the sound broke up the tension enclosing them. 'Oh, well,' he answered, 'if I've got to go broke, what better way than that to do it?' He upended his glass and in two swallows the amber liquid in it disappeared, then he walked towards her, placing the tumbler on the dressing-table as he passed.

His hands on her shoulder, he stood her away. He said, 'Have I ever told you how much I love you, Clarissa?'

'No, *that* you have not! However, you *have* told me how much you wanted me.'

Again that low laugh echoed through the brightly lighted room, and Clarissa thought it sounded happy. Then Alexis was saying, 'Oh, yes, I wanted you! But for now I'm going to show you that I can combine both the love and the wanting.'

An index finger of one hand stroked across her cheek, along her throat, and down against the lace and ribboned

cleavage, then up the other way all over again. 'Oh, yes,'
came Alexis' voice, but the tone in it had changed, 'I
think I can promise you that I can blend both together
completely before this night is out.'

His arms tight, he swung her up as he had done earlier
and set her on the pillows. On the bed beside her, his two
hands went out and she was imprisoned between them.
Then, bending down, he lightly rubbed his lips over her,
saying, 'And a second thing I promise you. I won't be
going to sleep tonight until a lot of hours have flown
towards tomorrow.'

'But what if I do, Alexis? It's been a long day, you
know.' Clarissa was smiling as she put up a hand to lie
against one side of the tanned, handsome face.

'Oh, I don't think you'll want to do that, but then we'll
have to wait and see. But first . . .' He rose, and as he
went through the rooms clicking switches she saw the
cabin gradually fall into darkness until only the bedside
lamp sent out its illumination.

Then Alexis was back and, leaning over, he reached
across. 'And we don't want this either,' he said, and
another switch was pressed. She saw him looming over
her outlined only in starshine.

'Now,' he said, coming to lie outstretched beside her,
'what are we to do about this—what did you call
it—handful of material?' Fingers had swept down along
her entire form, sliding on thin, transparent cotton; they
swept up again and it was over her shoulders and dropped
on to the floor.

Not expecting it, unprepared, Clarissa opened her eyes
wide. Her lovely nightdress! It didn't deserve such
handling. But suddenly she had other things to think
about.

Fingertips were sending their message over bare, cool
skin, and Alexis' lips, following their passage, were giving

to nerves she had not known she possessed a warning of desire. She knew once that as his hand, fingers outspread, came to rest within the hollow of her hip, she had gasped, her entire body jumping. But even then there still only came again the slow heartbreaking caresses he was pouring over her. Unable to help herself, her body arched completely to him, and a husky gasping voice she didn't recognise said, 'Alexis . . .'

She did know somewhere far back in her consciousness that this slow, careful lovemaking down the dark passage of time was his way of showing her that love, and wanting, could be combined.

Even as that thought had slowly penetrated a mind only aware of another dimension, Alexis' lovemaking changed. Now he was directing at her a passion, a blazing desire that brought body to body, and she felt herself flying, trying to reach a pinnacle with grasping hands, knowing she would die if she didn't capture it.

Later, a minute, an hour, or an aeon, she found herself lying quietly within Alexis' arms. She said, in a voice clouded with emotion, 'Alexis . . .'

'Sh. Go to sleep,' she was told.

Already almost over the borderline of it, Clarissa contentedly closed her eyes. But the other eyes above her remained wide; lips beneath them curled in a reminiscent smile. Then that smile turned into an expression of satisfaction, as Alexis eased the form of the sleeping girl more carefully into his embrace.

And as a random gleam of starshine found its way into the dim, silent room, those lids too fell shut. The hours had gone and it was tomorrow as Alexis had said it would be; but to the two sleeping forms lying there entwined, tomorrow was another day.

HARLEQUIN
Romance®

Coming Next Month

#3049 ANOTHER TIME, ANOTHER LOVE Anne Beaumont
Laurel Curtis isn't planning to change her status as a single mother. A
traumatic experience with one man was enough. Connor Dyson, an Australian
property tycoon buying the lease on her flat, has other ideas—like taking over
Laurel, too!

#3050 PARTNERS IN PASSION Rosemary Carter
Teri comes back to her grandfather's African game farm where eight years
ago, before she had to move with her parents, she had loved Rafe—and
thought he loved her, too. Now Rafe greets her as a stranger.

#3051 FACE VALUE Rosemary Hammond
Christine agrees to do one last modeling job before she changes careers. John
Falconer, however, has devised the assignment of a commercial for his
company simply to meet her—and he offers Chris another proposition entirely.

#3052 HOME FOR LOVE Ellen James
When interior designer Kate Melrose is hired to redecorate an unknown
client's home, she falls instantly in love—with the house! But she soon falls
even harder for its owner, the handsome, irascible Steven Reid.

#3053 THE CHAIN OF DESTINY Betty Neels
When Guy Bowers-Bentinck comes to her rescue, Suzannah, alone in the
world and without a job, is forced to accept his help. Not that she wants to be
beholden to such an infuriatingly arrogant man!

#3054 RASH CONTRACT Angela Wells
Karis doesn't welcome the reappearance of Nik Christianides in her life—
reawakening tragic memories she's spent years trying to suppress. Now,
though, she has to listen to him because he has a way of replacing what she
had lost.

**Available in May wherever paperback books are sold, or through
Harlequin Reader Service:**

In the U.S.
901 Fuhrmann Blvd.
P.O. Box 1397
Buffalo, N.Y. 14240-1397

In Canada
P.O. Box 603
Fort Erie, Ontario
L2A 5X3

**In April, Harlequin brings you the
world's most popular romance author**

JANET DAILEY

No Quarter Asked

Out of print since 1974!

After the tragic death of her father, Stacy's world is shattered. She needs to get away by herself to sort things out. She leaves behind her boyfriend, Carter Price, who wants to marry her. However, as soon as she arrives at her rented cabin in Texas, Cord Harris, owner of a large ranch, seems determined to get her to leave. When Stacy has a fall and is injured, Cord reluctantly takes her to his own ranch. Unknown to Stacy, Carter's father has written to Cord and asked him to keep an eye on Stacy and try to convince her to return home. After a few weeks there, in spite of Cord's hateful treatment that involves her working as a ranch hand and the return of Lydia, his ex-fiancée, by the time Carter comes to escort her back, Stacy knows that she is in love with Cord and doesn't want to go.

**Watch for *Fiesta San Antonio* in July and
For Bitter or Worse in September.**

JDA-1